Molly's Promise

ORCA
YOUNG
READERS

Molly's Promise

SYLVIA OLSEN

ORCA BOOK PUBLISHERS

Library and Archives Canada Cataloguing in Publication

Olsen, Sylvia, 1955-
Molly's promise / Sylvia Olsen.
(Orca young readers)

Issued also in electronic formats.
ISBN 978-1-4598-0277-3

I. Title. II. Series: Orca young readers
PS8579.L728M64 2013   jc813'.6   C2012-907461-6

First published in the United States, 2013
Library of Congress Control Number: 2012952947

Summary: When Molly has to break a long-held promise to herself, she finds her voice and reconnects with her mother, who left Molly when she was a baby.

MIX
Paper from
responsible sources
FSC® C004071

ANCIENT FOREST ™
FRIENDLY

Orca Book Publishers is dedicated to preserving the environment and has printed this book on Forest Stewardship Council® certified paper.

Orca Book Publishers gratefully acknowledges the support for its publishing programs provided by the following agencies: the Government of Canada through the Canada Book Fund and the Canada Council for the Arts, and the Province of British Columbia through the BC Arts Council and the Book Publishing Tax Credit.

Cover artwork by Ken Dewar
Author photo by Rob Campbell

ORCA BOOK PUBLISHERS
PO Box 5626, Stn. B
Victoria, BC Canada
V8R 6S4

ORCA BOOK PUBLISHERS
PO Box 468
Custer, WA USA
98240-0468

www.orcabook.com
Printed and bound in Canada.

16 15 14 13 • 4 3 2 1

This story is for Madison,
who makes us all want to sing.

Chapter One

Grade seven was turning out to be Molly's best year of school yet. Ever since September, when Murphy and the other boys from the tribal school had come to Riverside Middle School, her life had taken a substantial turn for the better. She never would have thought that a boy could be her best friend. But that was exactly what had happened.

Molly hadn't had many great experiences with girlfriends in the past. In fact, grade six had been a disaster when it came to friends. Now that Murphy was her best friend, it didn't matter so much what Paige, who thought of herself as the most gorgeous girl in the entire world, or Nell and the other girls, who dedicated their lives to agreeing with Paige, thought about Molly.

She didn't only have a new best friend. She had a whole new crowd. With Murphy came three other boys, Jeff, Albert and Danny. So being friends with Murphy meant that Jeff and Albert were her friends too. And even Danny, the other member of what was sometimes called the Formidable Four, was sort of her friend.

The Formidable Four had transferred from the tribal school, a First Nations elementary school about half an hour out of town.

At first, Molly had thought, "Formidable? How arrogant!"

That was before she saw the boys play soccer and realized *formidable* was the right word. They were soccer heroes. The Riverside Strikers hadn't lost one game since the boys joined the team. Jeff was the star midfielder, Danny was the star defenseman, and Murphy was the best goalie anyone had ever seen. With Albert on the sidelines helping Coach Kennedy inspire the players, Riverside was simply unbeatable.

Before Molly met the boys, she had never given soccer much thought. Now, watching their games and cheering for her friends was one of her favorite things to do.

The girls' spring soccer season was about to begin, and Murphy kept bugging Molly to sign up. "Come on. Put on the boots," Murphy said out on the field at lunchtime one day. He tossed her his old soccer cleats. "Let's see what you can do."

"I don't want to wear those," she said, turning her nose up at the thought of sharing boots with Murphy's sweaty feet.

He laughed. "If you're going to be a soccer player, you have to wear boots."

"Okay, okay." She stuffed her feet into the smelly boots.

"Over here." Murphy waved to Jeff, Danny and Albert to join them.

Molly felt clumsy at first, but before long she was passing the ball to Murphy and Jeff.

"Wow! The girl is good," Jeff said.

Molly dashed forward to catch up to the ball and send it on to Murphy.

"She's got wheels," Murphy said. He sprinted to meet her.

Danny stood on the sidelines, looking sullen. He hated it when anyone other than him got a compliment.

He also didn't think girls could play soccer. The truth was, he didn't like Molly very much. Worst of all, he thought the Formidable Four should be a boys' club and that Molly had no business hanging around with them.

"Let's see how fast she is," Danny said, running up alongside them.

"Is that a challenge, Danno?" Albert shouted. "Did I hear you taking the girl on?"

"I'm taking you all on," Danny said, strutting up the field.

Murphy kicked the ball to the side. "Okay, you're on." He flagged his arm to Jeff and Molly. "Dan the Man wants to see who's got wheels. Let's go!" Murphy hollered.

"I don't want to race you guys," Molly said. She was cold and already tired.

"You worried you're going to get beat?" Danny sneered.

"I don't care if you beat me," she said, bending over to untie the boots.

"She's going to kick your butt," Jeff said.

Molly hated competition. Who cared who could run the fastest? But Danny would never shut up if she refused his challenge.

She had no choice but to join the boys near the goalposts. Sometimes boys for friends were a pain. They never stopped competing—arm wrestles, push-ups, chin-ups, burping, whistling…you name it, the boys never quit comparing their boy skills.

"I don't want to run this race," she said.

"Murphy thinks you got wheels," Danny said. "Let's see how fast they are."

"Okay, okay," Molly said. "But I'm only running to shut you up."

Albert moved to the other end of the field to officiate. Molly was disappointed that Albert couldn't race with them. If he hadn't gotten leukemia and needed chemotherapy, he would have been better than everyone. Even though he was sick from his treatments, Albert still had his soccer moves. But now he had to concentrate on getting healthy. He had to beat his illness before he could play soccer again.

"The race will be from goalpost to goalpost," said Albert.

Jeff, Molly, Danny and Murphy lined up on the outside.

Albert hollered, "Ready, set, go!"

Jeff took off ahead of the others. Danny and Molly ran elbow to elbow. She thought, for a few seconds, that she should let him win. Then, almost without thinking, she shot in front of Danny and finished a few strides behind Jeff, with Murphy taking last place.

"Whoooaahh! Way to go, girl!" Albert shouted as the four racers caught their breath. He laughed. "I'm talking to you, Danno."

"Shut up, Albert!" Danny said, and then he suddenly began to limp. "I shouldn't have even run. My knee hurts."

"Oh, poor Danno's little knees." Albert snickered. "They just decided to hurt since he got whipped by a girl."

Danny took a swing at Albert. "I said shut up."

"Molly's fast," Murphy said. "What's wrong with that?"

"She's a girl," Danny said. "That's what's wrong with it." He turned to walk away and mumbled under his breath, "A white girl."

Murphy pushed Danny's back with both hands. "You shut up," he said, raising his hands as if he was ready to fight.

Danny stared at Murphy for a few seconds, and then he shot off toward the school without saying a word.

Chapter Two

The trouble with Riverside was that Molly didn't fit in with the First Nations kids, even though her dad was First Nation. And she didn't fit in with the white kids, even though her mom, whoever and wherever she might be, was white. In Riverside you were either First Nation or white. It was one or the other.

Nell, a tall blond girl, had been her best friend in grade six. But Molly wasn't Nell's best friend. Paige was. And Paige didn't like Molly one bit. In fact, Paige bullied Molly every chance she had. When Molly had told her dad about Paige's bullying, he went to talk to her parents, which only made matters worse.

It was hard for Nell and Molly to be friends. Paige had rules. She insisted her friends be 100 percent devoted to her. That meant Nell and Molly could be friends only when Paige wasn't around. Compared to Murphy, Molly had realized, Nell wasn't such a good friend after all.

Murphy stuck up for his friends, no matter what. And Murphy was half and half, just like her, except his mom was First Nation and his dad was white.

Murphy always said, "We're not half of anything, Molly—we're both. We're everything."

Since Murphy had become her friend, Molly was learning to fit in to both sides. Murphy lived on the reserve, but Molly lived in town.

Molly had lived with her dad since she was ten months old. He was tall, wide and brown, with a head of thick, black hair. Molly was short, narrow and pale, with fine, straw-colored hair and blue eyes. Her dad said that her looks were all Molly's mom had left her. Until Molly met Murphy, she had felt like she was from another planet. She hadn't felt like she fit anywhere, not even with her dad.

Murphy had laughed when Molly complained about not fitting in. "It's no different on the reserve," he said. "They wonder why I look like a white kid. Mom says it's all thanks to my dad."

Before the Formidable Four became Riverside's soccer heroes, the white kids and First Nations kids had stayed in separate groups. The First Nations kids had hung around the old tennis courts or the cafeteria. The white kids had pretty much had the run of the rest of the school. Molly, trying to avoid both sides, had spent a lot of time with her earbuds, listening to music on her iPod—her favorite thing to do in the whole world.

When Molly was younger, she was okay with it being just her dad and her. But after she had become friends with Murphy, she had gotten to know his mom, Celia. Now, more than anything else, Molly wanted a mom of her own. She scoured her house to find clues about her mom. But there was nothing—no pictures, no letters. There wasn't a trace of her. When she asked her dad about her mom, he either got mad or ignored her.

"What's wrong, Moll?" he would ask. "For all these years it's been just you and me. Have I done something wrong?"

He hadn't done anything wrong. He was the best dad a girl could have. But she wanted a mom.

"No, Dad," she said. "You're the best dad ever."

Molly wanted to plead with him to tell her something, anything, about her mom, but she didn't want him to feel bad. So she quit asking.

Murphy understood how Molly felt, because all he got from his dad was a card on his birthday—sometimes. Murphy called his dad a no-show. He said that since he had never had any other sort of dad, he had gotten sort of used to it.

But all Molly could think about was the day her mom would come home. She could almost feel her mom's arms around her, hugging her for the first time. Sometimes Molly longed for her mom so much her stomach hurt. She would get excused from class and lie in the school medical room, staring at the pictures of nurses on the wall and wondering if one of them was her mom.

At night Molly would lie in bed and imagine her mom singing and telling her stories. She'd slip in her earbuds and listen to old-time singers, imagining she was listening to her mom. Molly knew she was making it up, and the whole thing was kind of crazy. But she needed to believe her mom was with her.

Chapter Three

In spite of Danny's nasty mood and Molly's preference for watching games rather than competing in them, the race had got her thinking that joining the girls' soccer team might not be such a bad idea. She was faster than she thought, and with a pair of soccer boots that fit she could pass the ball and probably even score.

But soccer wasn't exactly what Molly wanted to do. She didn't tell anyone what she *really* wanted to do. It was a secret she had promised never to share with anyone except her mom. So she had to wait until her mom came home.

Lunch was almost over by the time Jeff, Albert, Murphy and Molly reached the school after the race. Danny and a crowd of kids inside the foyer were crammed around the notice board. Molly stood on her toes and caught a glimpse of a large poster tacked on top of the other notices. It read:

CENTRAL VALLEY YOUTH TALENT
COMPETITION
Do you dance? Do you sing?
Are you a slam poet?

Danny read the poster. "So you think you can dance?" He jumped around pretending to dance. "Spare me the pain of watching all the try-hards from this school," he said. "It's going to be a freak show."

Murphy looked at the poster and said, "Do they really think Riverside has talent?"

"Maybe they're thinking about the soccer field," Jeff said, simulating a shot on goal.

Molly ignored the boys and read the small print.

Date: March 12
Place: Central Valley Community Arts Center
Time: 2-5 PM
Ages: Grades 6-12

Sign up by February 28

Registration forms are available at Riverside Middle School and Central Valley High School

Cash prize of $500 and a trip to Winnipeg to compete in the Canadian Youth Talent Competition

There were only two weeks to sign up and another two weeks to practice.

"We should put on the soccer boots," Murphy said. He dodged from side to side as if warming up in net.

"Hey, Molly, did you read the poster? How cool is that?" Nell appeared out of the crowd. "Paige is going to dance. She's got a mega-good chance."

Paige arrived, followed by Dede and Fi. She looked over Molly's head, making an obvious effort to ignore her. Molly was easy to miss. She was at least a head shorter than Paige.

"Come on, Nell," Paige said. She shot a deadly glance at Molly and turned to her friends. "I've got to decide on a dance and get my costumes and…how am I going to wear my hair?" She pulled the elastic band from her ponytail, releasing her hair in a cascade of golden waves. "What do you think? I love my hair down, don't you?"

"No kidding," Fi said. She brushed her fingers through Paige's hair. "If you got it, girl, use it."

"You are soooo right," Dede said as the girls disappeared back into the crowd. "I just love the way your hair…"

When the bell rang, Molly reread the poster carefully, noting the time, the place, the entry fee and the names of the judges—Leroy Macpherson, Tiffany Terrell and Magpie.

She silently rolled *Magpie* around on her tongue. Magpies, Molly had discovered in Earth Sciences class, were one of the most intelligent animals, even though they were only little songbirds. They could sing for more than an hour without stopping.

Molly took another look at the poster. Pictures of dancers floated around the edges, making it look like it was advertising a dance competition, not a talent show. Under the writing in the center of the poster was an image of a hand holding a large microphone. She shivered.

"Come on, Molly!" Murphy called from the end of the hall. "We can't get started without you."

First block after lunch was Foods class. Molly, Jeff and Murphy were cooking partners. Today they were making pizza.

"What's up with you, Moll?" Murphy said when the pizza was finally ready to eat. "You're pretty quiet." He shoved a huge bite in his mouth.

"What do you guys think about the talent show?" she asked.

"Huh?" Murphy grunted as he wiped his mouth with his sleeve.

"I said, what do you guys think about the talent show?"

Jeff laughed. "One fish, two fish, red fish, blue fish, maybe I'm a poet?"

"No way, Jeffman." Murphy made an *X* with his arms. "You got real talent. You should suit up and do a solo show with a soccer ball. The audience could count one kick, two kick, good kick, great kick."

"Now that's real talent." Jeff smiled. "Singers and dancers won't have a chance against a skill like that."

"It's a great idea," Molly said. "No one else would even think of it."

"I was just kidding," said Murphy. "No offense, Jeff, but I don't think you'd be very entertaining."

"But it's a talent," Molly said. "Everyone would think it was great."

"No freaking way. I'd probably flub it after five or six kicks," Jeff said. "Murph should sing. Or Danno could dance. Yeah, he could wear a tutu."

Murphy and Jeff were laughing so hard, Molly decided not to say any more about the talent competition.

"Did I hear you guys making fun of my dancing ability?" Danny pirouetted over to their table and dropped into a chair next to Molly. "Molly is the one who should dance," he said, appearing friendly. Then, with a mean look, he said, "She should stick to what she's good at."

"At least I can dance better than you," Molly said.

Murphy said, "Why don't you just leave her alone?"

Danny got up, slammed his chair against the table and went back to his own cooking group.

"Thanks," Molly said. "I don't care if he doesn't like me, but he doesn't have to keep rubbing it in."

Chapter Four

Having PE first thing in the morning made Molly tired just thinking about it. She plunked herself on the bench and untied her shoes.

Paige strolled around the change room in her bra and undies as everyone put on their gym strip. "I'm so crazy scared," she said, and she placed her hands over her mouth. "There are going to be dancers from grade twelve, and I'm only thirteen. That's not even fair."

The way Paige swaggered around the room with next to nothing on made Molly cringe and admire her at the same time.

"You don't have to worry. You look sixteen," Dede said. Dede had turned thirteen a few weeks earlier but could pass for sixteen any day, especially with all the makeup she caked on her face.

"You will look divine," Fi said.

"You can do it," Nell said. "No worries."

Nell was taller than the other girls, and prettier, too, as far as Molly was concerned.

Paige swooshed her head from side to side. "I am the reigning provincial dance champ," she said, pulling on her T-shirt. "I can beat anyone my age, no worries—but what about the older girls? Oooh." She stepped into her shorts. The length of her legs amazed Molly.

"Do you know anyone else entering the talent show?" Molly quietly asked.

Paige swung around and glared at Molly. "Maybe you," she said and laughed. She did a little tap-dance routine and stamped both her feet, edging forward until she was less than an arm's length away from Molly. "Did you hear that, girls? Molly is going to dance. I thought she just liked to play with boys." Paige swiveled around and sashayed out of the room.

Molly's voice faltered. "I'm not going to dance."

Nell said, "It's going to be so great. I'm going to be Paige's stage manager."

"Sounds like a blast," Molly said.

Loni, one of Albert's cousins, sat nearby, pulling on her sneakers. She didn't look one bit impressed by any of them, and said, "So what? Paige may have longer legs than the rest of us, but her ego is a size super-extra-large."

"I hope she falls flat on her face," said another girl.

"She may be a great dancer," Molly said, taking time to fold her clothes, "but she doesn't have to be so mean."

The trouble was, no one could ignore Paige. Molly included. Not only could Paige somersault, vault, cartwheel, handspring and rope-climb better than anyone, but she also looked better than everyone else while she was doing it.

In the gym, Molly watched Paige float from one tumbling station to the other and wondered how genetics could get everything in one body so perfect. Paige's mother must be beautiful, Molly thought.

Molly considered her own awkward performance and abandoned her talent-contest dream. She thought of her own mom. She must be short, with a serious lack of talent, at least in the dancing and gymnastics departments. And she was definitely not beautiful—not if, as her dad said, Molly looked like her.

After school, Molly said to Murphy, "No one is even going to compete against Paige. Everyone is so sure she's going to win."

"Talent competitions are dumb, anyway," he said. "Who'd get up on stage in front of a bunch of judges just so they can tell you that you suck?"

"Would you go and watch?" Molly asked.

"No way," he said and shook his head. "It would be painful. A bunch of rock star wannabes up there on the stage making fools of themselves."

Molly slumped over and put her elbows on her knees.

After a minute, Murphy said, "What's up with you, Moll? You've been quiet all afternoon."

"Nothing's up," she said.

"Well, you're not saying much."

"So what? Can't I be quiet sometimes?"

"Hey, no worries—don't bite my head off," he said. He put up his hands as if to defend himself. "Who cares about Paige, anyway? You could beat her at soccer any day."

"I don't want to play soccer."

"What do you mean?" Murphy asked. "What do you want to do? Dance?" He laughed.

"No, I don't want to dance. And quit being such a jerk."

"Then what?" he asked. "Be a rock star?" He pretended to be an announcer. "And now, put your hands together for the Amazing Mollgirl."

"You're not funny, Murphy." Molly couldn't speak anymore. She picked up her backpack and headed toward home.

Murphy grabbed his bag and followed.

For the first time since she had met Murphy, Molly started to cry.

"Hey," he said. He reached a hand toward her and then yanked it back. "Hey," he repeated.

She wiped her nose on her scarf. "Sorry," she said.

"No worries," he said, relieved Molly's tears had stopped.

Molly said, "I wish I had my mom." But that wasn't what she really wanted to say.

"Yeah," Murphy said.

"And…"

"And?" Murphy asked.

Before she had time to answer, Jeff and Albert charged out of the school's front doors.

"We have a game tomorrow," Jeff said. "Central Avenue Cougars think they can beat us this time."

Albert said, "They've got a new goalie from Vancouver. Some kid called Han Tihn. He hasn't been beat. I hear he's only had two goals scored on him this year."

"I've only had four," Murphy said, defending his record. "And one should never have been called a goal."

Molly pushed past the boys and up the sidewalk. Let them talk about soccer—she wasn't interested.

It was a dark afternoon. Tattered, angry-looking gray clouds raced across the sky. Molly usually liked the wind. But today it was cold and hard, and it bit into her skin like puppies' sharp teeth. The only relief she got was on the straight stretch of the road where Mr. Smedley had his cabin. Giant Douglas-fir trees were lined up close to the pavement. It was calm there. Molly listened to the sound of the wind. It had a rhythm like high-pitched voices and violins. She thought of the words the voices might be singing.

Molly wanted her mom, but that wasn't the reason she had cried. It was the promise she had made to herself that was upsetting her. She knew she wasn't going to be able to keep it for long, and she wasn't going to be able to keep it a secret either. Molly felt as if something was bursting inside. Her secret was going to explode.

Chapter Five

"Hey, Moll," her dad said when she got home.

"Hey, Dad."

Molly went into the bathroom and splashed water on her face. After she dried off, she looked in the mirror. She knew what she wanted to say to her dad. Now she had to find the courage.

She sat at the table and said, "There's a talent show in town next month."

Her dad took a noisy slurp of coffee.

"I want to sing at it."

His face went pale. His brow furrowed.

"Why shouldn't I?" she asked.

"I'm just surprised," he said. "I've never heard you sing. I mean, I didn't even know you sing."

"I love music, Dad. You're the one who turns the radio off."

"I like it quiet." The look on his face became more troubled than surprised.

"I sing all the time," Molly said. "I imagine in my head that I can sing just like the singers on my CDs. I practice in the shower and walking home through the trail."

She stopped. What she had said wasn't exactly true. She had never sung a note in her life—not out loud. "Well…I don't sing, exactly. I sing in my head," she said. "I never sing the words out loud."

Her dad's forehead creased again. "You sing in your head? Not with your voice?"

"Yeah," she said, recognizing how strange it sounded.

"Why?"

"Because…" She had told him enough. "Because that's just what I've always done. But now I want to sing out loud, and I want you to listen to me."

"Here? Now?" he said.

"Yes. Here. Now." She knew if she thought about it for even half a second longer, she would lose her confidence. "I want to know if I'm good enough to enter the competition."

"Don't you need music or something?"

"No. I sing without music all the time."

"You sing without your voice all the time too."

"*Dad*."

"Okay, honey."

Molly got up and stood in front of the kitchen sink. "You look more nervous than I am."

"I might be," he said.

The truth was, Molly was terrified. She wasn't afraid to sing. At least, she didn't think so. She was afraid to break her promise. Molly couldn't remember when she had made the promise. It was a long time ago, and it weighed on her.

Mom, I have a gift for you when you come home. I promise that you will be the first person to hear me sing.

The trouble was, her mom hadn't shown up, and Molly couldn't wait any longer. Her voice had to come out now, and that meant she was going to break her promise.

Molly straightened her back. She took a deep breath so the air went into her belly, filled her chest and came up into her throat.

But Molly's voice had never come out of her mouth or entered a room before. It had only bumped off the walls of her imagination. All of a sudden she wasn't sure whether her vocal cords could hold even one note, never mind carry a whole song.

"I'm ready, Moll," her dad said.

A breath of air sent shivers down her legs and arms. Then she heard music. Her toe began to tap. She opened her mouth and started. *"Summertime, and the livin' is easy, fish are jumpin' and the cotton is high…"*

She kept her eyes closed and pretended her mind was her only audience. At first her voice wavered, but after a few moments, it filled the room. It grew louder and stronger until she felt as if she were going to explode. When she finished the last chorus, she opened her eyes.

Her dad was shocked. "Wow, Molly," he said. "You can sing."

"Are you sure?" she asked, stunned by the sounds she had made. "And do you think I'm good enough to sing in a talent show?"

"There won't be another kid in that show that can hold a candle to your talent, honey." He pulled her onto his lap. "You sound like a pro."

"Well, I have been singing ever since I can remember. Just not out loud."

Her dad frowned and chuckled at the same time. "That's crazy, girl."

Molly told him all the details about the talent show. She explained how Paige had set herself up as the one to beat. She told him she was afraid to tell anyone at school that she wanted to enter the contest. The boys would tease her. The girls would make fun of her. And Paige would make her life absolutely unbearable.

"Could I enter the contest without telling anyone? Could I just show up and sing?" she asked.

"You're tougher than that, Molly," he said. "If you want to enter the competition, go through the front door."

The truth was, now that Molly had sung out loud, all she wanted to do was sing some more. She didn't really want to compete—not with kids from school listening to her, especially Paige and the other girls.

"Paige might be able to dance," he said, "but you are a star. There is no doubt about that."

Molly climbed off his lap. "Thanks, Dad."

Later, as she lay in bed, Molly replayed her singing over and over in her mind. She loved how her voice had filled the room. If only her mom had heard her.

Molly had broken her promise. She had given her mom's gift away.

"Mom, I am so sorry. I couldn't keep my voice inside any longer. It just had to come out."

She said sorry over and over again, hoping her mom would forgive her.

As Molly fell asleep, she heard Billie Holiday singing "Summertime." Although she had been dead for seventy years, Billie's voice pulsed through Molly's body.

In the morning, Molly made a new promise.

"When you come home, Mom, I will sing just for you," Molly said. "It will be just you and me."

Her second promise didn't feel exactly right, but it was the best she could think of. Her voice had always been her gift to her mom. It still was. Now if only her mom would come home and get it. One day, Molly thought, my mom will come home and ask,

"What is your big surprise, Molly? Where's the present you promised me?"

Molly would take a deep breath and sing. Her mom would be amazed. "Molly," she would say, "I had no idea. What a wonderful gift. Thank you so much for sharing it with me."

Molly felt a little better after she had made the new promise.

The trouble was, now Molly didn't know what to do about the competition. One minute she wanted to enter, and the next minute she didn't.

When she got out of bed, she found an envelope on the kitchen table. On the front it said, *Here's the registration fee. Go for it, Molly. You can do it. I love you, Dad.*

Chapter Six

Molly was dozing off during the morning announcements until Ms. Clarkson, the principal, said, "Forms for the Central Valley Youth Talent Competition will be available in the office during lunch hour. We need your fee and your form, fully completed. Don't dally. The competition is just weeks away."

It was raining hard at lunchtime. Murphy was in the gym with the rest of the team, practicing for the game after school. Molly sat on the bleachers watching— and thinking about whether to pick up a registration form. A crowd of grade-eight girls stood nearby.

"Darcie's going to tap-dance," said a blond girl with a purple, feathered hair band.

"Paige is in my dance studio," another girl said. "She's pretty good."

"She thinks she's going to win," said a girl with heavy eye makeup. "Have you seen her? She struts around like somebody crowned her the Queen of Talent."

"She is soooo conceited," the blond girl said. "But what about Devon? That guy can sing AND play guitar. He's a star, baby. The next Mr. Bieber. What do you think, girls? Let's put it together for our very own Devon Dempster."

A chorus of laughter, sighs and coos came from the girls all at once.

Molly's face burned. Why had she thought she could sing in the competition? Devon was not only the best-looking boy in the school but also talented at everything. He could walk onstage with his hands in his pockets and say his name and he'd win the competition.

Someone said, "Mica can sing. Anyone know if she's entering?"

"Probably. She takes singing lessons," said the girl with the eye makeup.

Molly didn't want to hear any more. She swiveled around, jumped off the side of the bleachers and sped out of the gym. In the hall she ran into Paige and her friends.

"What does it say? What does it say?" Dede asked, flapping her hands hysterically.

Fi held up a piece of paper and squealed. "It says, *Write the winner's name here*. Paige Nelson!"

Paige grabbed the form. "Settle down, girls. It's just the registration. You're putting too much pressure on me."

Molly didn't have a chance to slip away without being noticed. She sat on a bench outside the gym doors.

"Hi," Molly said quietly to Nell when their eyes met.

"You should come down to the multipurpose room. Paige is going to practice. I'm her stage manager," Nell said. "Did I tell you that already?"

"Yeah, you did," Molly said. "I'm going to the soccer game."

"It's pouring," Nell said.

"I've got an umbrella," Molly said. She thought getting drenched at a soccer game would be more fun than watching Paige parade around on the stage.

Paige hollered from down the hall. "Nell, what are you doing, girl?"

"Gotta go," Nell said and ran to catch up with the others.

"Yeah, of course you gotta go," Molly said. She sat on the bench and looked down the hall toward the office. Maybe she should just forget the registration. The soccer team interrupted her thoughts as the players spewed out of the gym.

"We are gonna beat those suckers," Danny shouted, high-fiving the other boys.

The only team that had a chance of beating the Riverside Strikers this year was the Central Avenue Cougars. They were only two points behind Riverside in the standings. With two games left in the regular soccer season, the boys could clinch the title with a win this afternoon. A loss would give Central Avenue a chance to tie it up.

"We're going to win it," Murphy said when he saw Molly.

"I know," Molly said, "but aren't you worried?"

"Do I look worried?" Murphy asked, puffing his chest out.

"Sort of," she said. His noisy teammates jostled in front of them. "The whole team sounds pretty hyped."

Murphy had started playing soccer in grade six, five years after most of the other boys. Now that he was the starting goalie, people thought he was the most important player on the team.

"We have to win this afternoon, and everyone's looking for me to play a big game," he said.

"Ouch," Molly said. "That kind of pressure must hurt."

Murphy said, "No worries. All pressure is self-inflicted." He laughed. "I can handle it."

The truth was, Murphy loved competition. He even loved the pre-game jitters. He had told Molly after the last game, which was a 3-0 shutout, that tough competition made him nervous but also made him play better. The better the opposing team, the better Murphy played.

Molly loved competition too—as a spectator. The very idea of competing in something herself made her stomach hurt.

After school the rain stopped, and a chilly sun came out and brightened the field. Murphy's mom had brought two chairs and a blanket for her and Molly to share.

Molly's shivering lips slurped hot chocolate from a thermos. "Mmm, thanks," she said. "This hits the spot."

Soon a crowd of Riverside fans had lined one side of the field, and Central Avenue fans lined the other. The game got off to a quick start. Eli made a pass that bounced off a Cougar defenseman and went into the net off the goalpost. The crowd erupted. A lucky fluke for the Strikers. The excitement died down as the game turned into a running match—the Riverside boys were chasing the ball, not playing it. After a Cougar defenseman kicked the ball into his own net, the score at half time was 2-0 Strikers.

"Murphy said you-might join the girls' soccer team," Murphy's mom said. "He told me about the race. You beat him by a mile. Way to go, girl."

"Not quite a mile," Molly said. "But I don't think I want to play soccer."

"Really?" she said. "You love soccer."

"I think I make a better fan than a player."

They watched without talking for a few minutes.

"What would you like to do?" Celia asked.

Molly pulled the blanket up around her ears. She couldn't bring herself to speak the words that were bubbling up inside.

Celia looked sideways at her and said, "Moll, what do you have stashed away in that head of yours?"

Molly wanted to tell her about the talent competition. She wanted to tell her that she wanted to sing.

"I want to see my mom," Molly said. "I want to know about her. When I ask Dad, he either gets mad, changes the subject or looks sad. How come?"

"I don't know why he does that," Celia said and looked back at the game.

The Cougars' fans exploded. The players huddled and high-fived in front of Murphy's net.

"Did you see what happened?" Celia asked.

"No," Molly said. "I can't believe I missed it."

Murphy emerged from the crowd, holding the ball. He rolled it to the referee. The score was 2-1.

"Hey, Moll, I'm sorry about your mom," Celia said. "How about I talk to your dad?"

"Sure, thanks," Molly said.

"But that's not everything, is it?" she said.

Molly took a deep breath.

Finally the words came out. "There's a talent competition in town," she said. "I want to enter. But I also don't really want to. I don't want to compete. I just want to sing."

Once Molly started to talk, she couldn't stop. "Paige is going to dance. A lot of grade eights are entering." The words flooded out. She told Celia about the competition, her dad and the boys. "I want to sing more than anything." She stopped for a moment, then added, "Other than seeing my mom."

Celia's jaw slackened and her eyes opened wide. "Wow, honey," she said. "Thanks for sharing that with me. I didn't even know you sang."

"I don't," Molly said. "I mean, I don't sing to anyone but myself, with my mouth closed. I mean, I don't sing out loud. Except for once, when I sang to Dad."

Celia bit her lip as if it was she now who didn't know what to say. "He must have been surprised," she said.

"I think I surprised myself as much as him," Molly said. "I've listened to my voice in my head, but I didn't know it would feel that good to sing out loud."

Celia laughed. "Okay, Moll. That's a bit crazy, girl. But I hear you."

Their conversation ended when the Cougars charged into Murphy's zone. The Striker defensemen were scattered across the field. Molly and Celia threw off their blankets, jumped up and screamed, "Danny! Avtar! Where are you guys?"

The Cougar players passed the ball in front of the net, up the wing and then back across the back line.

Molly clenched her fists. If they scored, the game would be tied.

Murphy's eyes never left the ball. Danny and the other Striker defensemen were losing ground as the play moved closer and closer to Murphy and the net. Molly swallowed the lump in her throat. The Strikers left way too much to Murphy, as far as she was concerned.

"Come on, Danny!" she hollered. "Get with the game."

A Cougar player passed the ball to his wingman. A tall lanky boy trapped it, took a stride and wound up. Murphy moved to the right in anticipation. The striker kicked with brutal force, sending the ball to Murphy's left. The crowd went silent for a second. Molly watched the ball soar through the air. As it did, Murphy quickly changed his position. The tips of his fingers connected with the ball just inside the goalpost. He curled his hands around the flying rocket and dropped like a stone onto the ground. Both teams charged in front of him and halted a short distance from the pile that was his body and the ball.

Albert appeared next to Molly. They grabbed each other and jumped up and down, screaming, "Murphy, Murphy!"

The few minutes left in the game resulted in another goal for Riverside. The deflated Cougars took no more shots on Murphy. His big save had given the Strikers the confidence they needed to take control of the play.

With the win, the Riverside Strikers were the Valley Cup champions for the first time in fifteen years. Murphy's final, spectacular save had also won him the most valuable player award.

"Wow," Molly said after the crowd had settled down. "That was way too stressful for me. I don't know how Murphy does it."

Chapter Seven

"Good morning, Riverside students." Ms. Clarkson's voice was always particularly cheery on Fridays. "Spring soccer starts in a few weeks. The girls' team is looking for players. It's a good time for anyone who hasn't played before to try out. And we have had a great response to the talent-show registration. But today is your last chance to get a form. They must be returned to the office, with the fee attached, by Monday noon."

Molly felt inside the pocket of her jacket. The twenty-five dollars her dad had given her was there. She had thought about giving it back to him. After Murphy's last game, she'd decided that competition was okay for Murphy, but not for her. She would have to find another place to sing.

"This morning I want to have a discussion about the talent show," Mr. Bahli said when the announcements were finished. "Has anyone in this class entered?"

Veronica, a worried-looking girl who sat in the far corner of the room, put up her hand and nodded.

"Veronica?" Mr. Bahli said, looking surprised. "Wonderful! What's your talent?"

"Piano," Veronica quietly said.

"That's fantastic!" he said, walking down the aisle toward her desk. "Have you performed before?"

"Yes," she said. "I've been doing piano recitals since I was four years old."

"Really! Tell us about them."

"Some are good. Some aren't so good," she said. "During the Christmas holidays, I went to Toronto to compete for a place in a summer music school. Last week I got an acceptance letter in the mail."

"Wow! That's so great," Molly said. "Good for you."

It was easy to imagine Veronica as a concert pianist. She had delicate features and slender hands, with perfectly groomed oval nails. Veronica looked like the kind of girl whose parents could afford piano lessons.

"So what do we think about competition?" Mr. Bahli asked the rest of the class.

"It's all about winning. Second place is first loser," Danny said. "Like on Wednesday. The pressure was on, and we kicked the Cougars' butts. We rocked."

"I don't expect to win the talent competition," Veronica said, louder than before. "A singer or dancer will win. I need to practice, and the competition will help me with my performances. I just want to play the piano the best I can."

Molly didn't care about winning. But she wasn't calm like Veronica. When she thought about the competition, the butterflies in her stomach turned into swarms of bumblebees.

"So," Mr. Bahli said, "everyone has their own reason for competing."

Now that Molly had heard her voice out loud, she loved the way it sounded. And she loved the way she had felt when her dad was listening. Now all she wanted to do was sing. The competition would give her that chance, just like Veronica said.

At lunchtime, Molly charged out of the classroom alone and ran down the hall to the office. "Can I have a registration form, please?" she asked.

The secretary said, "Sure thing. What are you going to perform in the show, Molly?"

"Sing," she said, surprising herself with her confidence. She didn't notice Fi and Dede sitting in the hall.

The girls burst into laughter. "Sing?" Dede said.

Fi clasped her hands over her ears. "Will we have to listen?" she asked.

"No, you don't have to listen. But you do have to be respectful, and that was rude," the secretary said.

Fi whispered something in Dede's ear, and the two of them burst into laughter again.

Molly took the form and shot out the door. Part of her wanted to tear it up and never think about the competition again. But part of her wanted to show the girls that she *could* sing. Still another part of her wanted to hear her voice in the huge auditorium at the community center. Then she thought about her mom and felt a twinge of guilt. Even though she had made another promise, Molly still worried about singing in front of a crowd before she sang for her mom. It didn't feel right.

Molly was in such a muddle that she almost ran into Murphy in the hallway. She hid the form behind her back. "Where did you come from?" she asked.

"What do you mean? I've been looking for you." He peered around her shoulder. "What are you hiding?"

"Nothing," Molly said. "Just a form from the office."

"What form?" he asked.

"I'll tell you if you promise not to tell the other boys."

Murphy looked confused.

Molly knew that having a boy as a best friend had its problems. Murphy didn't understand secrets. He and the boys didn't have any rules about what they said to each other.

"It's a registration form for the talent contest," she said.

"It's a what?" Murphy asked.

"You heard me," Molly said, holding the form in the air as Murphy grabbed for it.

"What are you going to do?" he asked.

"Never mind." She stomped into the cafeteria.

Murphy followed her. He peered over her shoulder as she filled in her name, age and address. Under the heading *Talent*, she wrote, "*SINGING*."

"Singing!" Murphy said. His eyes bulged like someone had pinched him. "You are going to get up onstage in front of a ton of people and sing?"

Molly turned her back so he couldn't see what she was writing. "What's wrong with that?" she asked.

"What's wrong with that? You don't know how to sing."

"How do you know?"

"I know 'cause you've never said a word about singing. And you talk about everything."

"I don't know if I'm any good," Molly said, "but I've been singing my whole life. I've just never let the sounds come out of my mouth." She pulled out the twenty-five dollars, grabbed her completed form and stood up. "Come on. Let's drop this in the office," she said.

"I can't believe it," Murphy said. "I thought I was your best friend. And I thought girls told their best friends everything."

"You don't know anything about girls," Molly said in a huff.

"Hold on a minute," Murphy said. "Did you just say you sing but you never open your mouth?"

"Yeah," she said, walking away. "That's what I said."

"How do you do that?" he asked.

"I listen to myself in my head," she said.

"You listen to yourself sing, but you don't make a sound?" He looked at her like she was out of her mind. "Why do you do that?"

"Because…" She paused. She knew she'd never be able to explain her secret promise. "Because that's just what I do."

"So because you sing in your head, silently, you think you can sing in a talent competition?" Murphy asked.

"Yeah. I mean, no. I mean, I'm not sure."

Murphy said, "You are crazy, Moll."

"Yeah. I know."

Molly sat down on a bench in the hall. Murphy's reaction was only half as bad as the other boys' would be. She didn't even want to think about what they would say.

"Okay," he said as he dropped onto the bench beside her. "Fill me in. What are you talking about?"

Molly told him how she had sung for her dad and that it was the first time she had ever heard her own singing voice. She told him how her dad had been shocked and had left twenty-five dollars for her on the table the next morning.

"Have you been practicing with him?" Murphy asked.

"No," Molly said. "He doesn't like music."

"How are you going to win a competition if you don't practice?" Murphy asked. "If you have never sung for anyone? That doesn't make sense. Music in your head doesn't mean you can sing."

"Yes, it does. You don't understand."

"You're right," Murphy said, folding his arms across his chest. "I don't understand."

"Then come over after school, and I'll sing for you. If you think I suck, I won't sing in the competition."

"Murphy, my man." Paige sauntered up the hall with her friends. She flipped her ponytail with her fingers and said, "Did you know your Molly girl is a singer? She thinks she's the next Selena Gomez."

Fi said, "Is she trying to recruit you to be her talent manager? As if she has any talent." She sat herself down on Murphy's knee and flirted. "I'd like you to be my talent manager."

Murphy stood up, almost toppling Fi to the floor. He turned toward Paige and said, "Yeah. Molly's a singer, and I'm her manager. Look out, Selena—Molly is about to arrive."

Paige glared at Molly and then batted her eyes at Murphy.

"Well," she said with a sappy smile. "Tell your friend she's got some serious competition." Her smile turned to a sneer. "She's gonna be laughed off the stage."

Murphy said, "No one will be laughing Molly off the stage. You heard that first from me."

Paige's face turned bright pink. She gave a fake giggle and then she and her friends moved on.

"Holy cow," Murphy said. "You better know how to sing or I just buried myself."

"Thanks, Murph," Molly said.

"Come on," he said. "We've got work to do. First of all, we better leave that form in the office. Then I better figure out how to be a talent manager."

"Don't worry about it, Murph," Molly said, setting the paper on the counter. "You don't have to do anything for me."

"Yeah, I do," he said. "This is a competition."

The secretary said, "Good luck, Molly."

"Thanks," Molly and Murphy said together.

In the computer lab, Murphy Googled "talent manager." He scanned website pages. "Okay, so I'm supposed to deal with promotions, photography, how much you get paid, performances. As well as the business of singing, lessons, practices and... your image."

"You better quit now, Murph," Molly laughed. "Now you're the one acting crazy."

"I'm serious. It says lots of talented people never get heard because they don't have good management. It says good management is as important as good talent." Then he paused and added, "Well, almost."

Molly shrugged and said, "You don't even know if I can sing."

Chapter Eight

After school, Murphy and Molly walked home together.

"I'll text Mom and see if she can pick me up from your place later," he said.

"Thanks," she said. "For sticking up for me."

"I didn't have much choice," he said. "Now we have to deliver."

"You don't have much faith in me, do you?" she said.

"It's not about faith. It's about getting up in front of tons of people and singing."

After Molly had eaten a bowl of Cheerios, and Murphy had eaten two, they went into the living room.

"I'll put on the music," Murphy said.

"I don't use music," she said.

Murphy sat down on the sofa and scrunched a pillow on his lap. He looked afraid—as if someone was going to give him some very bad news.

"Calm down. This won't hurt," she said. But her stomach felt as if someone had stuck a knife in it. She closed her eyes and took a deep breath. Murphy disappeared. Her foot began to tap, and she started to sing.

Summertime, and the livin' is easy
Fish are jumpin' and the cotton is high...

When she had finished the song, she opened her eyes. Murphy was staring at her as if he had seen something supernatural.

Molly's heart pounded against her ribs. She waited for his assessment. "So?" she asked. "What do you think?"

"Where did that music come from?"

She put her hands on her chest and said, "It's in here, and for some reason it won't stay inside anymore. It has to come out."

On a normal day, Molly knew, she looked small and insignificant. There wasn't anything wrong with how she looked, but she wasn't pretty in the normal sense of the word. Some of the girls had changed a lot since grade six. Molly wasn't one of those girls. Her hair was stringy, her clothes were plain, and she had no hips or breasts. She still looked like a little girl.

But when she sang, she felt bigger—taller. She had to be. It was impossible for a sound like that to come from a small girl.

"Why haven't you told anyone?" Murphy said, looking confused. Molly looked different. He wasn't sure quite how. Older...stronger.

She took a deep breath. "Ever since I can remember, I've sung to myself—in my head. My voice was my secret, and I promised myself that my mom would be the first one to hear me sing. I wanted to give that to her—it was my gift. So I was waiting for her to come home." Molly swallowed hard. "But she took too long. It had to come out. I couldn't wait."

Murphy nodded.

"I broke my promise when I sang for Dad," she said. "So I had to make another promise. When my mom comes home, I am going to sing for her—just her and me."

"She'll like that," Murphy said. He was quiet for a couple of seconds. Then he jumped up and said, "Okay, Amazing Mollgirl, we've got work to do."

"Really? So you think I should sing in the competition?" she asked.

"Of course," Murphy said. "Trouble is, I'm not sure what to do first. Maybe I should ask Paige." He laughed.

"That's not funny," Molly said and punched him good-naturedly on his arm. "Don't you *dare* talk to her about this. Don't tell *anyone*."

Murphy looked at Molly. "The first word from your new manager is, get over it. If you're going to be a singer, then people are going to hear you sing. It's not a secret anymore."

"Murphy!" she said.

"Molly!" Then he added, "You know I'm right. Your mom will understand. You can still sing for her—just the two of you. She'll love it."

When Murphy went home, Molly worried about her promise. The problem with promises was that they were so hard to keep. She had broken her first promise, and there was something wrong about her second promise. It felt as if her mom would be getting a secondhand gift. She hoped Murphy was right and that her mom would understand. If Molly wanted to sing, people would hear her. The idea both terrified and excited her.

As soon as the boys jumped off the bus Monday morning, Molly knew Murphy hadn't kept his promise not to tell.

"Amazing Mollgirl," Albert said. "Can I have your autograph?"

Jeff jumped off the bus next and said, "Molly, you are going to be a star."

Danny followed Jeff. "I hope you're not singing stupid songs from some old dead singer," he said. "Who's going to want to listen to that?" Obviously, Murphy had told him about Molly's favorite song, "Summertime."

By the time Murphy got off the bus, Molly was furious.

"You promised," she said. "Why did you have to tell them?" She turned and stomped toward the school.

Murphy and Jeff ran to catch up with her. "It's okay," Jeff said. "We're going to help you."

"Oh, sure you are," she said, looking at Jeff through watery eyes. "I don't need help like yours."

"Yes, you do," Murphy said. "You need an audience to practice in front of." He turned to the others. "Billie Holiday might be dead, but she's still famous. She started singing when she was a teenager. She never had any professional training. The songs she sang are perfect for Molly's voice."

Molly looked at Murphy in amazement. "How do you know so much about Billie Holiday?" she asked.

"I Googled her," he said. "Mom and I watched as many of her YouTube videos as we could."

"You got your mom involved?" Molly asked.

"Mom said she'd be your costume designer," Murphy said. "And by the way, Moll, I didn't promise I wouldn't tell anyone. You asked me not to tell—that's different."

"Thank your mom for me," Molly said. "But I don't need a new outfit."

"Oh no, you don't need nothing—no practice, no costume, no help—'cause you are soooo good," Danny said.

Albert told Danny to shut up, but then he said, "Danno's right, Molly. How do you expect to win if you won't let anyone help you?"

"I don't care if I win," she said. "I just want to sing for people."

"That's not good enough," Murphy said. "You are a great singer. It's a cop-out to say you don't care about winning."

Murphy usually had a way of setting Molly straight without getting her angry. This time it didn't work.

"It's not a cop-out," she said. "You don't understand."

Murphy and the boys shrugged their shoulders.

"Don't ask me what she's thinking," Murphy said.

"I told you she's crazy," Danny said.

Maybe I am crazy, Molly thought, if I want to sing but I don't want anyone to hear me. Why am I entering the competition? Why did I break my promise to my mom? It was better when I sang to myself.

Chapter Nine

"Good wonderful morning, Riverside," Ms. Clarkson said. "Fourteen talented Riverside students have entered the Valley Talent Competition. Way to go. Clarissa Eng, a dance teacher from Vancouver, will be in the multi-purpose room at lunch today. She will talk about how to make the best of your performance. All the contestants and their managers are invited to attend. Bring your lunch and listen up."

Murphy gave Molly a thumbs-up from two desks in front of her. She frowned, shook her head and mouthed the words, "I don't want to go."

She imagined Paige and her friends hogging Clarissa Eng's attention. And besides, Molly couldn't think of one thing a dancer would know about singing.

Paige can win, for all I care, Molly said to herself. But the truth was, Molly hated the thought of Paige winning. She hated looking at Paige's fake smile. The only thing she would hate more would be Paige's real smile if she won the contest.

After the announcements, Murphy said, "It's just what we need."

"It might be what *you* need, Mr. Manager. I just want to sing," Molly said.

"You listen to your manager, Amazing Mollgirl. You aren't just going to sing—you're going to win."

Molly knew Murphy didn't understand. She wasn't amazing, and she didn't need to win. She needed to sing. Her voice had been trapped for too long. It felt so wonderful to let it out. But Murphy was her best friend, and he wanted to help. So she needed to let him.

"Okay, okay, okay," Molly said reluctantly. "I'll try and win the competition."

Some things you do for yourself, some things you do for your friends, and that's all right, Molly thought.

As soon as the lunch bell rang, Murphy flew out of math class with Molly chasing him.

"Hold up, you two," Ms. Clarkson said.

They skidded to a stop.

"You must be excited, Molly," she said. "I heard you are quite the singer."

"You're right," Murphy said, keeping his distance from Molly's fist, which she had clenched. "Molly sings like a star."

"I can't wait to hear her," the principal said. "But slow down in the hall."

"I can't wait to give you a beating," Molly said to Murphy as they continued down the hall. "How does she know how I sing?"

Murphy stopped outside the multipurpose room to let some other students through the door in front of him.

He gave her an official look. "Molly," he said, "if I am going to be your manager, you have to be manageable. And right now you, girl, are impossible."

Molly wasn't sure if Murphy was actually angry or playing manager.

"You signed up for this thing, not me," he said. "I'm going to help you. But when are you going to get it through your thick head that you are in a contest? There's going to be an audience. People are going to hear you. They are going to talk about you. When people hear you sing, they are not going to believe a voice like that came from a kid like you. You are going to win."

"What are we waiting for then, Mr. Manager?" she said with as much determination as she could muster. She led him to the front row. Albert and Jeff sat behind them and Danny plunked himself down next to Molly.

When Clarissa began to speak, Murphy pulled out a notepad and jotted down her suggestions.

"Are you kidding, Murph? You're writing notes?" Paige called from a few seats away.

"I'm her manager and we're going to win," said Murphy.

Paige giggled. "I want you for my manager."

"Sorry," he said. "I've got a client."

After Clarissa had finished, the boys and Molly huddled around Murphy. He held his notepad up. "I've got some good stuff."

Jeff said, "Okay, team, let's listen to the coach."

"Since when did this become a team?" Molly asked.

"Since now," Danny said. "If you're going to do it, you better win. You've got one chance to take this game."

"This isn't soccer," Molly said. "You guys don't get it. All I'm going to do is sing, once—that's it."

"That's all you're going to do—sing," Murphy said. "But it's a competition, and that's the part we know about. And when you compete for something, you compete to win."

"WINNING ISN'T EVERYTHING. WINNING IS THE ONLY THING!" the boys shouted.

Albert nodded. "That's why we're a team, Moll," he said. "You aren't singing in your head anymore. You're singing for judges."

"Listen," Murphy said, and he shook his notepad as if to call order. "Here's what you need to do. Number one, remember your audience and forget about them at the same time. You are there to entertain, and the audience will help you do that."

Murphy continued reading from his list. "Number two, enjoy yourself—at least, *look* like you're enjoying yourself. Number three, treat the microphone as if it's your best friend. Number four, every once in a while take a look at your manager—that's me. He'll give you confidence." Murphy laughed. "Number five, remember you are performing mostly with your face. Your face will win or lose it for you."

"My face," Molly said. "Are you kidding?"

"Really. It's your face that communicates with the audience and the judges." Murphy shook the notepad again. "I'm not finished."

By the time Murphy got to number seven, Paige and the girls, plus several other competitors, were crowded around him, listening. "Practice, practice, practice, until you know your piece so well you don't have to think about it."

"Is that all?" Molly asked. "Are you sure there aren't a hundred other things I need to remember?"

"Yeah, there's one more thing," he said. "Play to win."

"Murphy!" Molly shook her head. "Stop all the pressure."

"Clarissa said the performer who is the most convincing is going to win. That's a quote," he said. "You will convince everyone you should win because you love to sing, Mollgirl."

Paige said, "I think you have the wrong client."

Dede and Fi started to laugh. "There's no contest," said Fi. "Did you hear what else Clarissa said? Style? Confidence? Skill? Doesn't sound like Molly to me."

"Does to me," Murphy said.

Paige smiled. "Well, good luck with that, Murph. But if you want a winning client, you know my number."

"You need more than a manager, *Plague*," Danny said. "If you think you can beat Molly, you are in for a big surprise."

Before Paige could argue, Clarissa said, "Hey, come on, kids. Don't ruin the competition."

"Then tell Paige to shut up," Danny said as Paige pasted a big fake smile on her face. "She's the one slagging our team."

"We're just kidding, Danny," Paige said in a syrupy voice. She turned to Clarissa. "Clarissa, thank you so much for your help. Are you one of the judges?"

"The judges are listed on the poster," Murphy said.

When Clarissa walked out the door, Danny said, "It couldn't be any more obvious that you're just kissing butt."

Paige ignored him. "Molly should stick to soccer," she said. "I hear she can run and kick better than some guys around here. Or maybe Molly *is* one of the boys?" She tossed her head, and her ponytail swayed as she sashayed into the hall with the other girls shuffling behind her.

"You gotta beat that girl, Molly," Danny said.

When Molly got to the field after school, Paige, Dede and Fi were standing on the sidelines beside Albert. It was the last game of the regular season, with the Strikers playing the Searchlight Middle School Stars.

Ten minutes in, the referee called a penalty on the Stars' wingman. Free shot. The Strikers huddled for a few seconds before Jeff emerged and picked up the ball.

A Stars defenseman laughed out loud. "No worries," he shouted. "FN boys can't kick."

"First Nations boys can kick your butt," Danny said.

"That's enough," the referee warned, pointing his finger at the Stars player.

Jeff set the ball in its place, looked at the goalie, wound up and drove the ball high and over the left side of the goalpost.

"No worries, guys," Murphy shouted from halfway down the field. "Keep the pressure on."

Murphy had his eye on the ball. He looked at the field, at all the players, then back at the ball. He never lost his concentration, not for a second. He shifted from leg to leg and bounced on the balls of his feet. He slapped his hands on his arms. He was ready. All the time.

Molly threw her backpack down and sat on it. By the second half, it was a kick and chase game.

Riverside scored near the end of the game, but no one knew for sure who had made the goal. It wasn't until Jeff high-fived Avtar that the other players gave him a nod. When the whistle blew, the final score was 1-0 Strikers.

"Way to go," Paige squealed as she ran up to Murphy. "Good game."

"No, it wasn't," he said.

"But you won," she said. She stood in the middle of the boys as they picked up their gear. "And winning isn't everything—it's the only thing. Right, Murphy?" She turned to Albert. "With coaches like you guys, I'd be a winner for sure."

Danny threw his bag over his shoulder and said, "Come on, Murph. Let's get out of here. That girl makes me mad."

"*She's* not our problem," Murphy said. "The game didn't matter to our standings, but still, we played terribly. That's our problem."

"Hey, we won. We'd already clinched first place," Danny said. "What difference does it make?"

"Winning isn't everything. And it's not the only thing," Murphy said. "Not when you play a bad game."

"Geez, Murphy," Molly said. "You're never satisfied."

Chapter Ten

The next day when Murphy jumped off the bus, he was holding his notepad.

"Our first performance is after school at Grandma's place," Murphy said with an air of authority. "She said we could set up a stage in the living room."

"Murphy, ughhhhh!" Molly said.

Murphy ignored her. "Grandma says she's going to invite everyone."

If Molly could choose a grandma, Murphy's would be the one. She was always thinking up one crazy idea or another. Murphy lived downstairs at her house, and whenever Molly visited him, Grandma made sure to call them upstairs to eat fried bread or help her make chutney or hang lanterns from the ceiling.

The thought of singing for Grandma and everyone on the reserve terrified Molly. Singing in front of a huge crowd at the Community Arts Center wasn't as scary as that. But Molly decided not to argue if Grandma was involved.

After school, when Molly and the boys piled out of the bus at Grandma's house, Mousetrap, Murphy's scruffy white cat, was waiting for them on the street. His uncle Rudy leaned against his car in the driveway.

Grandma stood on the front steps, wiping her hands on her jeans. "It's about time," she hollered. "We're almost ready inside."

Molly and the boys said, "Hi, Grandma!"

"You're lucky I didn't have time to tell everyone." She laughed. "There's going to be standing room only as it is."

Molly picked up Mousetrap. He was the kind of audience she liked.

Inside, Grandma had pushed the dining room table into the corner and covered it with food—chips, tomatoes, apple pie, fried bread and jam. By the window, she had put a piece of plywood on top of some blue recycle bins to make a stage.

"It's safe," she said, climbing onto it. "See?" She jumped up and down. "I tied them together."

She had pushed the sofa to the edge of the living room and brought in kitchen and patio chairs and some stools from the basement.

"How many people are coming?" Molly asked. A large lump was forming in her stomach.

"More than will fit in this place," Grandma said. She was pushing the chairs together, cramming in as many as possible. "It's a fine-looking venue for your first performance, don't you think?"

It was too late for Molly. As her dad often said, the cat was out of the bag. Once Murphy became her manager, she didn't have much say in what happened. Her dad had heard her sing, Murphy had heard her sing, and now the boys would hear her sing, along with, from the looks of it, everyone else from the reserve that Grandma could stuff into her "venue."

"It looks fine, Grandma," Molly said.

She thought about her promise. She had to remind herself that it was okay to sing for everyone because one day her mom would come home and she would still have a gift for her.

Grandma greeted people at the door. "Help yourself to something to eat," she said. "Then grab a chair. This is a sold-out show."

People jostled around the crowded room.

Molly plunked herself on the corner of the stage. Murphy sat beside her. "I didn't know she was going to do all this, Moll. Really, I didn't," he said, his mouth full of bread. "But it's ideal."

"It's not ideal, it's terrifying," Molly said. "And don't chew with your mouth full. It's gross."

"Well, this is the biggest audience we're going to get," Murphy said. He swallowed hard and said, "For now."

"Don't get any other crazy ideas," Molly said. "I'm doing this for Grandma and that's it."

Murphy stuffed more bread into his mouth. "We could use the Chief Morris Community Hall. Grandma could ask them," he said.

"Just stop now, Murph," Molly said. "This is getting to be too much for me. And I'm telling you, I don't want to see the food in your mouth."

"We're ready to start," Grandma said. "Put some food on your plates and sit down."

The cramps in Molly's belly and the thudding sound in her head reminded her that she had no choice. The people were there to hear her.

Grandma put her fingers in her mouth and let out an ear-piercing whistle. Within a few seconds, the noise had subsided and it was perfectly quiet.

"Now I have your attention," Grandma said. "If you can't find a seat, lean against the wall. You are in for the performance of your life." Grandma edged her way through the maze of chairs to the stage and climbed onto it. "We've done a lot of things in this living room, but this is the first concert."

Molly looked nervously around the room. There were people she recognized and some she had never seen before. She spotted a small woman with red hair and pale skin at the back of the room, half hidden behind other latecomers. Molly's stomach clenched. The woman didn't look First Nations. Molly thought of her own light hair and pale skin. She thought about how short she was compared to the other girls in grade seven. The lump in her stomach got caught in her throat when she tried to breathe. Maybe today *was* the day she would sing for her mom. But it wasn't the right time for that. There were too many people here.

"Hey, Gloria." Grandma pointed at the woman. "Don't hide there in the back. Come right up here. There's one more chair."

Molly's stomach churned.

"Wow," Murphy said. "Danny's mom. I never thought she'd come."

Molly's body felt weak. It almost hurt. Then she realized her dad wasn't there. Why hadn't he shown up?

"We are ready, Molly, my girl," Grandma said.

Molly was limp. Her head felt like it was floating above her shoulders. Her voice was trapped in her throat. All she could hear inside her head was a dull thudding behind her ears. There was no music.

She pulled herself up onto the stage next to Grandma and looked at the audience—at one face and then another. The people were smiling. They wanted to hear her sing.

"We are in for a treat this afternoon," Grandma said. "Our next Long Inlet star is about to be born on the stage." She hugged Molly and said, "Take it away, Molly Jacobs."

Molly took a breath and looked around. No one moved. She still didn't hear any music. She waited. She watched the crowd as it watched her. Suddenly she felt a faint rhythm in her pulse. And then, gradually, she began to hear music, as if an orchestra were playing in her head. Molly tapped her foot. She breathed deeply again. She found her note and began, *"Summertime, and the livin' is easy, fish are jumpin' and the cotton is high…"*

When she finished the song, the room exploded with applause. Uncle Maynard, her dad's cousin, stood up and clapped so loud with his big hands that it sounded like he was beating a drum. Before he stopped, Molly said, "That was a George Gershwin song that Billie Holiday sang. I love her music. Next, I'm going to sing a Patsy Cline song. She's dead, like Billie Holiday. But she's one of my favorite singers too."

Molly closed her eyes and began. *"I go out walking after midnight, out in the moonlight just like we used to do…"* As the words came out, Molly forgot about the audience and about Murphy. She didn't think about Paige or Nell or whether the other girls liked her. Molly sang and nothing else mattered.

At the end of the song, Molly opened her eyes and looked at the people cheering. Grandma wiped her eyes, and Murphy's mom blew her nose. Molly jumped off the stage and sat next to Murphy.

He stood up and shouted to the crowd, "Do you want one more?"

The people cheered, "More! More!"

Murphy said, "Come on, Moll, they want more."

"I don't know what to sing," she said.

"You must know tons of songs."

"I do, but I can't think, Murphy. Not here, with all these people," she said. "I'm not like an iPod."

When the clapping didn't stop, Molly slowly climbed back onto the stage.

The deafening sound gave her goose bumps. But she wasn't afraid. She was excited, and she liked being on the stage.

She stood quietly until the noise subsided. "I don't know what else to sing," she said.

Then, without thinking, she began, "*I want a hippopotamus for Christmas…*" Everyone laughed to hear a Christmas song sung in March. When she finished, she said, "That's all I have for you today."

Before she had even jumped off the stage, people crowded around to congratulate her.

"Oh my, what a big voice for a little girl!"

"You are going to win for sure."

"Where did you get a voice like that?"

"We're so proud of you."

"You're going to make Long Inlet famous, Molly Jacobs."

They kissed and hugged her. Molly had never been the focus of attention like this before.

Finally, Murphy held up his notepad and said to her, "Okay, when you are done hugging your fan club, we have things to talk about."

"Not now, Murphy," Molly said. "Can it wait?"

"Okay," he said. "But we gotta talk."

When the last person had gone, Molly was alone on the front porch with Grandma and Celia.

"The people who were here today are your family," Grandma said. She squeezed Molly's shoulders. "I want you to remember that when you are up there on the stage being famous."

Molly knew she would never forget. She loved how it felt to have family—a great big reserve family.

"And this is from Uncle Maynard." Grandma pressed a napkin into Molly's hand. Inside it was a roll of bills. "He said to buy what you need. It's on him."

"That's awesome," Celia said. "I volunteer to be your fashion consultant." She laughed, then teetered as if she were wearing high heels.

"Do I really need to dress up?" Molly asked, thinking how she hated wearing anything but old jeans and T-shirts.

"You have to look exactly the way you want, honey," Celia said. "But think about it. That money means you can try out some cool clothes. Why not?"

Molly hadn't thought about it that way.

"Or," Celia said, "it means you can get your hair cut, or get a manicure."

Molly spread her fingers out and looked at her grubby, ragged fingernails. She laughed. "Do you think a manicure would help me sing?"

"How about Saturday morning?" Celia asked. "We can go to town." She pointed to the napkin. "My guess is that you have enough for a great shopping trip. I'm going to chip in as well. And maybe you can scrounge a little from your dad."

Chapter Eleven

When Molly got home, her dad was sitting in his favorite chair, watching the news. She flopped on the sofa across from him.

"You missed some kind of crazy event at Grandma's house this afternoon," she said, covering herself with a blanket. "How come you didn't come?"

"I couldn't get off work early enough," he said, not taking his eyes off the TV.

"Even Danny's mom was there," she said. "Uncle Maynard gave me some money. I'm going shopping with Celia Saturday morning. She said she'd chip in and that I should scrounge something from you as well." Molly couldn't believe how brave she was being. She usually didn't like asking for money.

"Of course, honey," he said as he pulled out his wallet and looked at her.

"I wish you'd been there," she said. "At Grandma's."

"I'm sorry, Moll," he said, leafing through the bills in his wallet. "I support you, I really do, it's just that…"

"It's just that what?"

"It's just that I've been really tied up with work. I've got a lot of things on my mind. But here." He passed her five twenty-dollar bills. "Is that enough?"

"It's plenty," she said. "I wish Mom had been there today."

He swiveled his chair so that they were face to face. "Molly, we've talked about this. Why do you keep torturing yourself with dreams that one day she's going to show up?"

Molly stared out the window at the budding tree in the front yard. "I made a promise when I was little."

"And?" he prodded. "What promise?"

"I promised myself that Mom would be the first person to hear me sing. That's why I only sang in my head, to myself. Then you heard me, and then Murphy, and now everyone on the reserve," Molly said. "Pretty soon everyone will have heard me sing *except* Mom.

I broke my promise. But my voice couldn't wait for her. I just had to sing."

He said, "I'm sorry, baby. I really am. But I'm glad you decided to break your promise and finally sing."

Molly sat up. "I've made a new promise though," she said. "When I finally see my mom, I'm going to sing just for her. It's going to be the first thing I do when I see her. My voice—it's still a present for her."

Her dad looked confused.

"Thanks for the money, Dad," Molly said, changing the subject.

"Get something that makes you feel great."

She put the money into her pocket. "I've never gone shopping like this before."

"I'm sure you'll get the hang of it," he said.

Murphy's mom arrived at nine o'clock on Saturday.

"Trev, we'll be back around three, if that's okay," she said. "Unless, of course, you want to come with us."

Molly's dad laughed. "No, you two go ahead. I'll sit this one out," he said. "Happily."

"Your girl is going to be a star," Celia said, pulling a chair out and sitting down at the kitchen table. "Can you believe how she sings?"

Molly's dad said simply, "Yeah, I can."

He and Celia stared at each other for a moment in a way that made Molly realize she was missing something, something being said without words.

Molly stood in the change room, glaring at herself in the yellow dress Celia had picked out. She looked like a daffodil. She tore it off and looked at her scrawny feet, her thin, tube-like torso and the space between her teeth. She was nothing but a scruffy little kid. Her hair hung in strings over her flat chest. Her butt didn't even fill out her baggy undies. Her knees stuck out like giant knobs on her bruised legs. And, worst of all, hair had begun to grow under her arms, a pathetic announcement that one day she would be an adult. There were no other hints of maturing taking place, other than the greasy skin she had begun to notice around her nose. She got dressed, leaving the dress crumpled on the change-room floor, and tramped out of the store. "I hate shopping."

"Don't give up so soon," Celia said. "You have to get good at shopping. It's like anything else—you have to practice."

"Practice, practice, practice," Molly said. "I don't want to practice."

"Okay, then," Celia said. "How about we quit shopping for a while and find someone to do your hair?"

"I've never had my hair done at a salon," Molly said.

"You'll love it."

Molly concentrated on her face in the hairdresser's mirror. Her fine, straw-colored hair was parted in the middle and straggled down the sides of her face and over her shoulders. Her eyes were so pale, it was hard to tell if they were blue or green. Her skin was light, but compared to the woman in the chair beside her, Molly realized, she looked tanned. Boring—that's the best word to describe me, thought Molly.

"So, sweetie," the hairdresser said cheerily. She was a tall, lanky young woman with hair as black as shoe leather except for a shock of pink on top. "My name's Reggi. What do we want to do today?"

Molly shrugged.

Reggi turned to Celia. "What does Mom think?"

"She's not my mom," Molly quickly said, and then, worried that she had sounded snappy, added, "I mean, she's my friend's mom."

"Okay, friend's mom. What do you think?" Reggi asked.

Celia told Reggi about the competition. "So we need a winning haircut."

"Wow, cool!" Reggi said. "I've got a great cut for you." She explained that she was going to cut bangs, layer the body and blunt the ends. "How does that sound?" she asked.

Molly said, "Anything will be better than the haircuts Dad does."

When Reggi was finished, Molly swung her head from side to side. Her hair didn't only look great. It also felt great.

"Thanks," Molly said. "I don't look boring anymore."

Reggi stepped back and looked Molly up and down. "Girl," she said, "you are not even close to boring. You got something inside you that most of us only dream about. You go get it, do it, love it, feel it. Just sing, girl, sing."

Molly brushed a few hairs off her shirt and felt something changing inside. She flicked her head again and watched her hair slither and glimmer.

It wasn't easy, but finally Molly found clothes that were right—a pair of high leather boots, jeans and a red T-shirt. She and Celia found a screen printer, and on the front of the T-shirt they had *Sing Girl Sing* printed in black letters.

On Sunday, Murphy showed up at Molly's house after breakfast, carrying his notepad. "Less than a week to go," he said. "We have to rehearse."

"Morning, Murph," Molly's dad said.

"Ya, hi, Mr. J," he said, checking his list. "We haven't even decided what song Molly's going to sing."

"I think we all know she has to sing 'Summertime,'" her dad said. "The judges won't believe it."

"That works for me," Murphy said. "What do you think, Moll?"

"It works for me, too," she said. She felt good that her dad was taking an interest.

"And we haven't decided if she's going to sing a cappella or use music. What do you think?" Murphy asked.

"Let's go without music. No one else is going to sing that way," said Molly.

"Okay, no music," Murphy said firmly.

Molly's dad and Murphy sat on the sofa.

"We're ready," her dad said.

After Molly had sung, Murphy said, "Good. That was really good. Next time, think of us as the judges."

She sang it again, wincing slightly at the thought of competing.

"You didn't look as happy that time," her dad said.

Molly scrunched up her nose. "I wasn't," she said. "I don't like being judged."

Murphy said, "Get used to it. That's what this is all about."

"For you, maybe," she said.

"Okay. This time pretend we're the audience," he said.

Molly imagined hundreds of people watching her. She felt them breathing. No one made a sound in her imagination. No one moved. The more she sang, the closer they listened, until in the end they erupted like a flock of geese taking to the sky.

"Wow, Moll," her dad said. "I think you're ready. What do you think, Mr. Manager? How can she do better than that?"

"You're right, Mr. J. And I think she likes an audience better than judges." Murphy read his notes. "We need to check a few things. Clothing. Do you have something comfortable? Hair. It's awesome, Moll. Tickets. Mr. J, do you have a ticket?"

"Not yet," her dad said.

"No worries," Murphy said, digging in his pocket. He handed Molly's dad a rumpled ticket. "Grandma thought you might need one. She bought twenty tickets, or something like that. Everyone is coming early to get front-row seats. Molly's going to have the biggest cheering section there."

Molly stood next to Albert on the sidelines of the soccer field on Sunday afternoon.

"So, Moll," Albert said, tapping a ball with the toe of his boots. "Are we going to win?"

"I'm sure of it," Molly said, taking her eyes off the boys, who were practicing shooting on Murphy in the net. "We're a little weak on offense now that you aren't playing. But we've got Murphy—what else do we need?"

Albert slapped her lightly on the back. "I'm talking about the talent competition."

"Oh, that team." Molly nudged him back in a friendly way.

"Yeah, that team," Albert said. "Sorry I didn't make your practice this morning. These days I feel like crap in the mornings. It sucks."

Molly had been thinking so hard about singing and soccer that she had forgotten Albert had gone for another cancer treatment.

"And what about your team at the hospital?" she asked, noting the dark circles under his eyes and the grey color of his skin.

"The doctor said we're winning," he said. "Three more trips to Vancouver and that's it."

"That's it?!"

"Then I have to wait and see if the cancer is all gone."

Molly hated waiting. Waiting for a doctor to say whether or not you still had cancer sounded brutal. "Waiting must suck worse than anything," she said.

"I don't care about waiting so much," Albert said in a flat tone. "All I care about is not having any more treatments."

Molly didn't know what to say. She hadn't ever asked Albert what the treatments were like. He went down to Vancouver and then, after a few days, he returned, looking sick and tired.

They stood quietly for a few minutes and watched the boys drill the ball at Murphy.

"I have to win the game I'm playing," Albert said.

A lump formed in Molly's stomach. Albert had more pressure on him than she wanted to think about.

"I think you should sing to win as well, Moll," he said. "'Cause if you can, you should."

"I hear you," she said. "Thanks."

After a few minutes, Albert said, "Whatever you did to your hair, it looks cool."

Chapter Twelve

"Hey, Molly." Nell ran to meet her as she entered the schoolyard the next day. "Your hair. It's totally fantastic. I can't believe it's you. You look so…so…"

"So…so what?" Molly asked.

"So…fantastically cool," Nell squealed.

Molly laughed. "Settle down."

Nell reached out and stroked Molly's hair. "You look older. You look hot. Paige is going to be soooo jealous."

"Paige? Jealous? Of what?" Molly asked.

"You, of course."

"Me? Why?" Molly asked.

"Your hair, for one thing. Oh my gawd, no one will believe it's you," Nell said. "And your voice. I hear you can really sing."

"You are telling me that Paige, Miss Stunningly Beautiful, is going to be jealous of me because I got a haircut? Are you kidding me?"

"Yes, that's what I'm saying," Nell said.

Molly said, "Paige thinks I'm a pathetic nobody. Now I'll be a pathetic nobody who got a haircut. And neither of you guys have even heard me sing, so I don't know what you're talking about."

"Paige doesn't need to hear you. She's jealous because the guys say you are great."

"She never used to even look at Murphy and his friends until they became soccer heroes," Molly said.

Dede and Fi swiveled around and gasped when Molly entered the washroom. Before Molly had time to back out the door, Paige and Nell came in behind her. Molly was trapped.

"Hey, have you guys seen Molly?" Paige asked.

Fi and Dede said, "Huh?"

"Duh. Molly. You know—Molly, the little boy. She's trying to be a girl for a change. Now that she thinks she's some kind of jazz singer, she's got the hots for Murphy," Paige said.

The other girls fumbled with their ponytails.

"Yeah, we just saw her," Fi said. "She's got a fancy hairdo."

"She probably thinks it'll make her win on Saturday," Paige said. She threw her head back and laughed hysterically.

"She's just jealous of you, Paige," Fi said. She stepped in front of Molly and looked right past her, as if she wasn't there.

Molly's knees felt watery. When she turned to find a way to escape, she couldn't get her feet to move.

"She's going to totally embarrass herself this weekend," Fi said.

Paige shot a nasty look at Molly. "I'm terrified." The girls laughed. "I'm not kidding. I'm terrified she's going to ruin the whole show. She'll embarrass us all."

Molly headed for the door. "Excuse me."

To her surprise, Paige moved aside. As Molly passed, Paige bumped her hard with her elbow. "Don't think you can beat me, you little creep," she said.

Molly dragged her soggy legs into the hall.

Murphy was waiting there with his notepad and calendar. He had already marked that day's date with a giant X. "Five more days, Molly," he said.

"That's not long," Paige said, sauntering out of the washroom with the other girls behind her. "Does that mean you've decided to be my manager?"

Molly leaned against the wall and slithered down to the floor. She wished she had the strength to stand up and tell Paige to shut her mouth. But she couldn't move.

Murphy said, "I thought I said Molly." He turned to Albert. "Did you hear me say Molly?"

Albert laughed. "I heard you say Molly."

"Did anyone hear Murphy talking to Paige?" Danny asked.

Paige's face turned red. She swung around and saw Molly sitting on the floor. "Looks like your singer is a real winner, Murph. I'm giving you one more chance."

Murphy ignored Paige and said, "You okay, Moll?"

Jeff pulled Molly to her feet. Her legs felt like wet noodles.

"I'm okay," she said.

Paige strutted down the hall with Fi and Dede close behind her. Nell was pale and shaky. She put her hand on Molly's arm. "I'm sorry," she said. "That was horrible." Then she followed Paige and the other girls.

"I booked the stage in the multipurpose room for three o'clock tomorrow to practice," Murphy said.

"Do I have to?" Molly asked.

"Yes, you do. Forget those girls. They're stupid," Murphy said. "Tomorrow we'll have a stage and a microphone."

"Grandma had a stage," Molly said. She would love to forget the girls, but the competition was making that more impossible every day.

Murphy said, "But you need to practice with a mic. Plus Clarissa's going to be there."

After school the next day, Murphy and the boys were waiting for her when Molly arrived at the multipurpose room. And sure enough, Paige and the other girls lingered in the hall nearby.

"Oh, hey, Murph," Paige said, feigning surprise to see him. "What are you doing here?"

"We're on at three," he said.

Paige said, "I'm on tomorrow afternoon at four. You're invited." She pushed her hips a little closer to him. "If you want to watch someone worth seeing, that is."

Danny said, "Don't you ever quit?"

Murphy ignored Danny and Paige. "Okay, Moll, I googled using microphones, and I've got some stuff we need to go over."

"I'm listening," Molly said.

"The first thing is distance—the mic can't be too far or too close from your lips."

"Sounds good," Molly said.

Nell appeared in the hall. She walked past Paige and stood in front of Molly and Murphy. She waited for Murphy to finish and then she said, loud enough for everyone to hear, "Hey, Murphy, can I watch Molly this afternoon? Maybe I can help."

"Are you switching teams?" Danny asked.

"Yeah," Nell said. "I want to be on Molly's team."

"Nell, are you kidding?" Paige said. "You're *my* stage manager, in case you forgot."

Clarissa and Veronica came through the door. "Your playing is exceptional," Clarissa was saying to her.

"You might want to think of accompanying a singer sometime."

"Like Molly," Murphy said, overhearing the conversation. "That would be awesome."

"No kidding," Veronica said. "But let's wait until after the competition. Can I join you guys for Molly's practice?"

Murphy nodded. "For sure."

Chapter Thirteen

"Testing. Testing," Jeff said, tapping the microphone.

Molly sat on the edge of the stage with Nell. "Thanks for being here," she said.

"I'm so sorry, Moll. For everything," Nell said. "I'm soooo done with Paige, Fi and Dede."

"Are we all ready?" Murphy asked.

"Ready," several voices said.

"Then the show is all yours, Moll. Take it away," Murphy said.

Molly took her time. She held the microphone and breathed. It was quiet in her head. She looked out at the little crowd. They wanted her to sing. She waited until she heard music in her brain. She tapped her foot. She found the note. And she began to sing, *"Summertime…"*

When she finished, everyone jumped up and cheered.

Nell ran onto the stage and hugged Molly. "I can't believe it. Why didn't I know you could sing like that?"

Clarissa turned to Murphy and said, "No wonder you want to manage this girl. You've got a star on your hands."

"Okay," Murphy said. "Enough! We've got business to do here. That was great, Moll. But you have to use the mic more. And remember to stand straight. No slouching. How did you feel up there, Moll?"

She didn't want to say, "I love being on the stage." But that was exactly how she felt. "Okay," she said. She stepped forward and then back, trying to find the right distance from the microphone.

"Hang on, Moll," he said. "Clarissa, do you have any suggestions?"

"No," she said. "Well, I could say two things. Molly's a star performer, Murphy is a star manager, and these guys in the audience are a star audience. So I'm thinking you guys have a winning team. Let's hear it for all of you."

Everyone clapped.

Clarissa turned to Molly and said, "Just make that mic part of your body."

"We're ready when you are," Murphy said.

Molly put her lips up to the mic. "*I go out walking after midnight, out in the moonlight…*"

The sound reverberated off the walls of the multi-purpose room. Her voice surrounded her like a blanket. It was like the wind, the sun and a rainy day all wrapped in one. She could feel the sound and taste it. She could see its color and shape. It was as if she could reach out and touch her voice. She sang high and low, loud and soft. When she finished, she felt ten feet tall.

Clarissa shouted, "Oh! My! Goodness! Girl!" and the audience erupted.

"Sit down," Molly said. She pulled the mic out of its cradle. "I can't sing properly just standing up here. I need to move around."

Danny jumped onto the stage and pulled the micro-phone stand out of the way.

"Thanks, Danny," Molly said. She held the micro-phone in one hand as if she'd used one all her life. "Now, once more, Mr. Murphy Manager," she said.

She walked the stage as she sang. The music was alive—she was alive. She looked out into the dark room. This is for you, Mom, she thought.

On the way out, Veronica caught up to Molly and said, "You don't need me playing with you. You don't need music at all."

"But I'd love to try it sometime," said Molly. "It would be really fun."

Paige and the girls were standing outside the multipurpose room, talking in low voices. From their sullen faces, it appeared they had heard Molly sing. Normally Molly would have avoided them. But today she looked first into Paige's face, then into Dede's and then Fi's. They were all silent. And for some reason, the nasty things Paige might have been planning no longer mattered to Molly.

On her way home from school, Molly thought about her promise and felt okay. One day she would sing to her mom. Just like she had this afternoon.

Chapter Fourteen

"One more day, Riverside," Ms. Clarkson said over the PA. "I want all the competitors and their managers to meet in the multipurpose room at 12:15. I have a few announcements from the organizers."

By the time Murphy and Molly arrived, the room was almost full.

Nell shouted, "Over here!" Nell and Danny had saved some seats up front. Paige, Fi and Dede were seated a few rows behind them.

There were so many people in the room, it was hard to tell who were competitors and who were supporters.

When Veronica came in, Murphy squeezed over to make room.

"Thanks, Murphy," she said.

"Hello, hello," Ms. Clarkson said too loudly. She needed Murphy's help with the microphone. "Attention, everyone."

The audience quieted.

"Congratulations. You've all put a ton of work into this. Now, I want all the contestants up on the stage to introduce yourselves. Not just your names. Tomorrow you'll be asked to say a few words about yourselves."

Slowly the contestants lined up beside the principal. Veronica and Molly were the last ones onto the stage.

One by one the competitors introduced themselves.

Paige was fifth in line. She walked up to the microphone with a swagger, flipped her ponytail and said, "My name is Paige Nelson. I'm in grade seven. I go to Riverside, but of course all you guys know that already." She giggled. "Why did I say that? Oh, and I'm going to perform a jazz dance called *Dancing in the Streets*."

Paige was right—she needed Murphy to manage her. No one had taught her about stage presence.

By Molly's count there were three singers, three singers with guitars, seven dancers and one pianist. When it was Molly's turn, she took the microphone out of its cradle and said, "My name is Molly Jacobs. I am in grade seven at Riverside. I am really excited to get to sing Billie Holiday's version of 'Summertime' at this talent competition. Thank you all for coming."

Ms. Clarkson ushered the competitors off the stage after their introductions. "What a good showing, Riverside students!"

While Ms. Clarkson read the rules for the competition and Murphy wrote in his notepad, Molly gazed at the stage and thought about how wonderful it had felt to hear her voice echo through the room.

Murphy elbowed Molly. "You better listen to this stuff. Twenty-three kids from the valley have entered." For the first time, Murphy sounded nervous.

"Finally," Ms. Clarkson said, "we've just learned that not only will the winner receive a cash prize and a trip to Winnipeg, but Channel 2, which broadcasts across the entire province, is going to be at the competition tomorrow. The top three contestants will be filmed for thousands of people to watch."

Murphy jumped out of his seat. "Moll, did you hear that? You might be on TV!"

Molly froze. She thought about her promise. If she was in the top three, her mom might hear her on TV.

If that happened, her mom wouldn't have to come home to hear her sing. Molly felt numb. Why hadn't she been told this before? If she had known, she would never have entered the competition.

Finally Molly understood why her promise was so important. She wanted there to be a reason for her mom to come home. Without that, she might never return.

Molly's eyes welled up with tears.

Nell sat down beside her. "Moll, what's the matter?"

"Nell, my mom," Molly said between sobs, wiping her face with her sleeve. "She might hear me on TV."

"That would be so cool," Nell said.

"No, Nell," Molly said. "She can't hear me that way. I promised. I want her to come home to hear me."

Murphy sat down on the other side of Molly.

"A promise? What's she talking about?" Nell asked Murphy.

"It'll be okay, Molly," he said.

"No, Murphy, no. My mom can't hear me on TV. She'll have no reason to come home if she does." Molly got to her feet and ran out of the room.

Murphy and Nell followed her into the hall. She slid down the wall until she was sitting on her heels. She buried her face in her arms and cried. Murphy and

Nell kneeled beside her. Soon the boys, Veronica and Clarissa were gathered there too.

"What's wrong? What's wrong?" everyone asked at once.

"I can't sing in the competition," Molly said, sobbing.

"What are you talking about?" Danny said. "You're going to win."

Murphy told them about Molly's mom and frowned. "I don't really get it either."

After school, Molly and Nell waited for the bus with the boys.

"You quit just like that, Moll?" Murphy said. "Come to my place and talk to my mom. Maybe she can help."

"Okay, but I can't do it. I just can't do it," she said.

Molly felt like she was in a blender. Her words and feelings whirled around and turned into a thick, soupy clamor. She was dizzy and a little sick to her stomach.

When the bus stopped, Murphy jumped off and ran into his house. Nell and Molly waited outside. A few minutes later, he came out with his mom.

"Come on, girls," she said, opening the door of her car. "Get in. We're going to Molly's. I'm going to have a talk with Trev."

When they got there, Celia handed Murphy a twenty-dollar bill and said, "Take the girls for something to eat at the market."

"What did you say to her?" Molly asked as she followed Murphy and Nell down the path to the store.

"I told her about your promise, about the TV, about you crying, and I said you weren't going to sing. She went into one of her rages and said she was going to talk to your dad."

"I'm so sorry about all this," Molly said. "I'll try and sing. But I can't get in the top three. I just can't."

"I don't get it," Nell said.

"The problem is, Molly made a promise to herself a long time ago," Murphy said. "That's why she never let anyone hear her sing until now. She was saving her voice for her mom, so she would have something to come home to."

Nell still looked confused.

Murphy shrugged. "It makes sense to Molly."

"Doesn't someone know where her mom is?" Nell asked.

"I don't think so," Murphy said.

"That's crazy," Nell said, putting her arm around Molly. "I'm so sorry, Molly."

"I'm the one who should be sorry for getting everyone into this," Molly said. "I just wanted a reason for my mom to come home. If she hears me on TV, I won't have that anymore. It might sound crazy, but it's what I believe."

"I think I understand," Nell said.

"I don't think anyone really understands," Molly said.

They all stopped and looked back as they heard the front door slamming. Molly's dad had bolted from the house and jumped into his truck. Celia appeared in the doorway. "If you don't tell her, I will," she shouted after him.

The tires squealed as the truck took off and disappeared around the corner.

The kids hurried back and joined Celia on the front steps.

"What's going on?" Molly demanded. "What is it you're not telling me?"

"Your dad has to tell you the story, Moll," Celia said.

"Oh man. We have one day—not even that," Murphy groaned. "We could have won tomorrow."

"This is not about winning tomorrow, Murphy," Celia said. "It's about Molly singing. And singing, for Molly, is about her mom."

"I need her," Molly sobbed. "My voice is a gift for my mom. I've known it since I first listened to music and sang in my head."

"No, honey," Celia said. "Your voice is your mom's gift to you."

"What do you mean?" Molly asked.

"Like I said, your dad has to tell you the whole story," Celia said. "But I will say that your mom is the most incredible singer I have ever heard. Well, let me correct myself. Your mom was the most incredible singer I had ever heard until I heard you sing. You are even better than her. Way better. But you sound exactly like her. You even sing the songs she liked. That's why your dad can't stand to hear music. Your house was full of music when he lived with your mom."

And all of a sudden, things lined up in Molly's head. She had heard her mom's voice before. Of course she had. When she was a baby, she would have heard her mom singing.

"Where is my mom?" Molly asked quietly.

Before Celia could answer, the truck pulled back into the driveway, and Molly's dad got out. He joined them on the front steps.

"I was wrong, honey," he said, sitting down next to Molly. "Really wrong. I wanted to protect you, so I didn't tell you anything. It turns out you would have been better off if I had told you everything. Maybe I was trying to protect myself."

He looked at Murphy and Nell, then continued. "Molly could sing before she could talk. She'd follow her mom around. Oh my, Molly's mom could sing. And she was pretty—just like Molly. She was kind and gentle and strong—just like Molly too."

Molly didn't move. She had waited all her life for these words.

"But Angela had some real serious problems. She got into trouble with addictions—drugs. Before Molly was a year old, her mom was hanging out with bad people. I'm not going to go into the whole story, but when Angela went to jail, I promised myself I wouldn't tell Molly about her. I thought the best thing to do was pretend her mom took off."

My mom is a drug addict and is in jail? thought Molly. That couldn't be. She must have heard her dad wrong.

"I made a mistake." Her dad's face was pale. His arms were slumped at his side. "Angela's cleaned herself up, and she wants to talk to Molly more than anything in the world. I said no, not until she gets out of jail. I didn't want my girl to have to tell her friends that her mother's in jail."

He gave Molly a long hug. "Your voice is both a gift from your mom and a gift for your mom," he said. "I called her the other night and told her you were singing. She begged me to let her talk to you."

Molly asked, "Where is she?"

"She's on the mainland."

Murphy said, "Wow, Moll."

Molly's dad said, "I don't know how you can sing for her like you promised. We don't have time to get you there and back before the competition."

"How about on the phone?" Murphy asked. "Your dad could set it up. It could be like a preview."

"Murphy," Celia said, "stay out of this."

"It's okay," her dad said. "That's a good idea. What do you say, Moll?"

A million thoughts ran through Molly's head. She had imagined this moment a million times, but she hadn't pictured it like this. Molly tried to remember every word her dad had just said. "Did you say Mom wants to hear me sing?" she asked.

"More than anything."

"Can you phone her?"

"Sure. If you want me to."

"Okay," she said.

"Are you sure you're all right with this, Moll?" Celia asked.

"Yeah," Molly said. "I think I'm sure."

Ten minutes later, her dad called from inside the house, "Molly, come here."

Molly walked down the front hall and into the kitchen. She stared at the phone and thought about how many times she had wished her mom would call.

"It's your mom."

Molly took the phone in her hand and put it up to her ear as her dad left the room.

"Molly? Are you there?" The voice was familiar.

"Mom?"

"I hear you are going to sing for me, honey," her mom said. "I have waited a long, long time for this." Her mom's voice was low, and as steady as Billie Holiday's.

"Yeah, Mom. I'm going to sing for you," Molly said. She waited a few moments, until she heard the music in her head. "*Summertime, and the livin' is easy, fish are jumpin' and the cotton is high…*"

When Molly finished, her mom began to sing. "*I go out walking after midnight, out in the moonlight…*"

"Wow, Mom, that's my number-two favorite song. 'Summertime' is my number-one favorite."

"Me too," she said.

It was quiet on both ends of the line. Then her mom said, "Just sing, Molly. Sing. I'll watch for you on the news. Honey, I am so proud." She paused. "And Molly"—her voice was interrupted by sobs— "I'll be out of here in less than a year." Molly heard her suck up a deep breath. "But Trev says we can get together sometime before that." She paused again. "If you want."

A wave of anger rushed over Molly. Her dad had kept her away from her mom. This was all his fault.

As if reading her mind, and before Molly had a chance to speak, her mom said, "It's not Trev's fault, Molly. He was trying to do what was best for you."

Molly looked out at the porch, where her dad sat with Celia. Her mom was probably right. Either way, the waiting was over, and now Molly was ready to sing.

Chapter Fifteen

Molly couldn't sleep that night. She thought about her mom in jail. It was scary. Was she safe? What would the kids at school think? She had never heard about anyone's mom being in jail. But when Molly thought about her mom's voice, a wonderful feeling came over her. She heard music and started to sing. This time she didn't keep the sounds inside. Soon she was so excited about the competition, she couldn't keep still long enough to sleep.

In the morning, Murphy and his mom arrived early. Molly's dad doubled the pancake batter so there would be enough for everyone.

"Murphy," Molly said, "don't eat with your mouth open. It's disgusting."

Celia laughed. "Thank you, girl. Sometimes your manager needs to listen to you."

Murphy ignored them. "It's nine o'clock. We've got five hours to get ready," he said and checked his notepad.

"We've got to get to the hair salon," Celia said.

"Murph and I are going over to the community center to get a feel for the lay of the land," Molly's dad said.

"How are you?" Celia asked Molly when they were in the car.

"Okay. Fine. Great. Better than I've been since as long as I can remember," Molly said. "And thanks. For everything."

"For threatening Trev, you mean," Celia said and laughed. "He thought he was doing the right thing. But I've always disagreed with him about keeping Angela a secret."

"I think I understand what he was trying to do. I guess he did the wrong thing for the right reason."

Celia said, "Exactly."

"Now, at least, I don't have to worry about winning or not winning. I can just sing," Molly said.

After Reggi had done Molly's hair and makeup, she said, "I'll be there to watch you, girl. 'Cause you are going to knock them over."

Molly looked in the mirror on the way out of the salon. The reflection was older and a little more impressive than the girl she was used to seeing.

Every minute seemed like hours. When they finally arrived at the center, Molly said, "I'm going to walk around the park for a while and get ready."

First, she made sure no one was watching. Then she pulled out the information Murphy had printed on singing warm-ups. She stretched her neck, shoulders, fingers, jaw—everything. She made blowing motions and filled her cheeks with air. Quietly she made sounds. "Waaa, waaa, maaa, maaa, weee, weee, meee, meee, wooo, mooo."

She took a few deep breaths and shook her body as if she were a rag doll.

Molly was ready.

By the time she got back to the center, people were crowding around the parking lot and streaming in the doors. Inside, her dad, Grandma and Uncle Maynard were sitting in the front row. They had put programs on all the seats around them. Albert and Jeff were in the next row. Danny was chasing Nell up the aisle. Reggi sat alone a few rows behind them. Dede and Fi were there, along with crowds of kids from school and what looked like hundreds of other people.

"Over here," Murphy called in a panicked voice when he saw Molly.

"Your name tag is inside the waiting room, with a package of instructions. You need to be backstage in ten minutes," he said, motioning over his shoulder with his chin. "There are twenty-three contestants—fourteen from Riverside and nine from Central High. You're number twenty-two." A long table with a red tablecloth stood in front of the stage. Three laptops were on the table in front of three empty chairs.

"You all right?" Murphy asked.

"Yeah," she said. "Fine. You?"

"Good," he said. "Not really. This is worse than a soccer game. In a game, you have sixty minutes to win. In this competition, you have three minutes to do or die."

"I'm not going to die," she said. "I'm just happy I get to sing, and it doesn't matter if I win or not."

Murphy threw her an exasperated look.

"Stop," Molly said, holding her hands up in an *X*. "What I mean is, I can sing to win if I want. I'm not worried anymore about promises or secrets."

"Does that mean you're going to try to win?" he said.

"Yeah. If I can, I should," she said, thinking about Albert. "I've got no reason to lose anymore."

"You're crazy," Murphy said.

The hall was full. Molly's cheering section was huddled around Grandma. She was passing out signs that read *Sing, Molly, Sing*!

Molly headed backstage and scanned the group there. A woman clapped her hands and said, "Quiet, please, everyone. I'm Tina."

Molly hardly recognized some of the girls she knew, in their dance costumes and makeup. Paige wore a long-sleeved, bright yellow bodysuit and a flower in her hair. She looked beautiful.

"Quiet," Tina shouted again over the racket. "I know you're nervous and excited, but we have to focus."

The group grew silent.

"You all have worked with the sound people. Right? Your music is ready. Right?"

Everyone nodded.

"You have your numbers. Right? So you know your order. Three people at a time will be ushered into the holding area." She pointed to a small room offstage and to her right. "Keep track of your number. Be ready. I will call you when it's your turn. If you leave this room for any reason, let me know. If I can't find you in time, you could lose your turn."

Murphy whispered, "You aren't going to be onstage for at least an hour."

Tina said, "I want you to be respectful and polite."

The contestants paced around the crowded room. Murphy couldn't keep still.

"One last thing." Tina pointed to three people who were standing beside her. "I want to introduce your judges. Leroy Macpherson, Tiffany Terrell and Magpie."

Magpie was a surprise to Molly. She had expected him to be a rap singer. But he had curly silver hair down to his shoulders. He wore red canvas running shoes that seemed out of place with his suit and tie. His smile was friendly, as if he was looking at all his grandchildren.

Murphy whispered, "Magpie's as old as Grandma. I think that will work in our favor. He's going to like the song you're singing."

Molly was struck by a sudden wave of panic. Should she have picked something more modern?

Veronica interrupted Molly's thoughts. "I'm number fifteen," she said. "What about you?"

"Second to last," Molly said.

Tina said, "All support people must leave the waiting area now. Numbers one, two and three, please step into the holding room, and good luck to everyone."

Murphy held up his notepad. "Just one more thing!"

"No, Murph," Molly said. "Not just one more thing. You've done everything you can do. It's up to me now."

"I guess you're right," he said. "High five!"

He high-fived her and Veronica and then left the room.

"You are so calm," Molly said to Veronica.

"It's over now," she said. "It's like I've already performed. There's nothing more I can do. No more practicing. No more psyching myself up. So now I have nothing to worry about. That's how I look at it."

The girls counted down as each performer moved to the small room offstage.

When it was Veronica's turn, Molly gave her a hug. "Good luck," she said, then laughed. "It's not really about luck."

Veronica giggled. "Good music."

When Tina called Paige's number for the holding room, Paige looked like she was ready to burst into tears. She didn't look tough or intimidating without Dede and Fi. In fact, Molly felt sorry for her.

"Good luck," Molly said. She wanted to tell Paige to listen to the music, to let it in and let it calm her down, but she decided it probably wouldn't help much.

As Paige walked past Molly, she mumbled, "Thank you."

As one contestant performed, another was summoned, and the backstage area slowly emptied.

Finally, Molly's number was called.

"How are you?" Tina asked Molly as she and the final contestant entered the holding area offstage.

"Fine," she said. "Really fine."

Number twenty-one was a beautiful tap dancer. As the girl walked off the stage, the man behind the mixing table jumped up and rushed over to the announcer.

"Hold on," the announcer said into the microphone. "There's a little sound problem with the music. We can't find the music for the next contestant."

The announcer and the soundman talked back and forth. Then the soundman ran across the stage to speak to Tina.

"What's wrong?" Tina asked.

"I've got music for number twenty-three, but nothing for twenty-two," he said.

Tina looked at Molly with a mixture of anger and panic. "I thought everyone said their music was set up. You were supposed to make sure this didn't happen. Where is your music?"

"Inside," Molly said.

The soundman and Tina looked puzzled. They weren't in the mood to make sense of what Molly was saying.

Molly said, "I'm not using music. I sing a cappella."

"Really?" the soundman said in amazement. "With nothing?"

"Nothing," Molly said. "I'm sorry—I thought you knew that."

He was up on the stage by then. He grabbed the microphone and said, "Sorry, gang, my mistake. This next performer is making her own music."

Molly filled her lungs with air.

The announcer said, "Number twenty-two is Molly Jacobs."

Molly placed each foot carefully on the stairs. Her boots clomped across the stage.

She took the microphone out of its cradle and said, "Hello, I'm Molly Jacobs. I'm in grade seven at Riverside. Thank you all for coming. I'm really happy to be here to sing 'Summertime,' made famous by Billie Holiday, one of my favorite singers."

She looked out into the sea of people. In the front and to her right was a crowd of faces she recognized—Grandma and her relations from Long Inlet, Dad, Celia and the boys. When Molly saw Albert standing at the edge of the crowd, clapping his hands, she remembered what he had said and knew what she had to do.

She took a deep breath and said, "Mom, this is for you."

Molly smiled. She closed her eyes, and the audience disappeared. Her body filled with music, and she began to sing. "*Summertime, and the livin' is easy…*"

When she was finished, the announcer said, "Wow, that girl's got music."

Veronica met her offstage and grabbed her hand. "I think you've got it, Moll. That was unbelievable."

"Thanks. I wish I could have seen you. How did it go?"

Veronica said, "Great, but from the performances I saw, you're it."

Earlier, Molly hadn't wanted to think about winning, but now she imagined how wonderful it would sound to hear her name being called—as a runner-up, maybe.

After the last contestant had finished, the announcer said, "It'll be about ten minutes for the judges to come to a decision. Hold on to your seats. We'll have the winners coming right up."

The soundman blasted a mix of audio clips of everyone's performances into the crowd. The contestants, sweating with excitement, began to dance.

Molly was startled when she heard her own voice on the sound system. It sounded like her mom's had on the phone. Exactly.

It felt more like half an hour before the announcer jumped back up onto the stage. He grabbed the microphone and held up a piece of paper.

"It's all here," he said. "I have the names of the top five contestants in my hand."

The crowd screamed. The contestants gathered in front of the stage and joined hands to form a line. Molly grabbed Veronica's hand. When she turned to see who had picked up her other hand, Paige squeezed it and said, "You were amazing."

The announcer hollered, "Let's hear it again for all the contestants."

When the noise of the crowd had died down, he said, "Fifth place goes to"—and then he paused while the soundman played a drum roll—"Jason Lawson."

Jason jumped up the stairs to the stage two at a time. Earlier, Molly had mistaken him for a parent. He was as big as her dad and carried his guitar as if he were a rock star.

"Fourth place"—the announcer waited for the drum roll—"Margo McLeod."

A tall girl floated gracefully up the stairs.

When the announcer said, "Third place," Molly began to worry that she was too young to win.

Off to the side, she heard Grandma chanting, "Mollgirl, Mollgirl, Mollgirl."

Molly's skin felt too small for her body. Her blood was rushing through her veins so fast, she thought she was going to explode. She wished she didn't care about winning, like before, but it was too late. She squeezed Veronica's hand so hard, her fingers hurt.

The drum roll lasted what felt like forever. "Devon Dempster," the announcer hollered.

Devon jumped up onto the stage without using the stairs.

Molly sized up the three winners standing in a line behind the announcer. She tried to picture herself standing beside them, but she didn't fit. She was too small. Too young.

There were only two more spots and a lot of contestants who looked like winners.

"Second place…" The announcer stood back and motioned to the soundman. The drums rolled.

The crowd went crazy. Murphy was standing on his chair, waving his notepad in the air. Molly's dad was taking pictures with his cell phone. Albert had held his hands up to his face as if he was too scared to see what would happen next.

"M—" For a split second, when the announcer's lips formed the letter *M*, Molly's heart stopped. "Melanie Yang."

The beautiful tap dancer stepped behind Molly and said, "Excuse me."

Molly moved aside to let Melanie past. Her heart sank. She had let herself imagine being in the top five.

"Are you ready, Valley people?" the announcer asked. He stood back and let the sound of the drums fill the hall.

The audience was on its feet. The announcer took the mic and tried to drown out their screaming. The remaining contestants had huddled so close together that Molly could hardly move.

"Quiet now. Get ready for the moment you all have been waiting for," the announcer shouted. He waited until the crowd had calmed somewhat.

"The winner of the Central Valley Youth Talent Competition iiiiiisssssssss Mmmmmolly Jacobs!"

Molly didn't know how she got to the stage. Later, Veronica said that she and Paige had pushed her toward the stage and then the line of performers picked her up and carried her up the stairs. Molly found her feet and walked to the announcer, who high-fived her so hard that she almost fell over. He draped a blue sash over her head and handed her a large envelope with a gold rosette on the front.

The soundman played a track of Molly singing. It was Billie Holiday. It was Mom. It was Molly, and it was wonderful.

Acknowledgments

Thanks to Maddy, my lovely granddaughter. You are truly an inspiration. Orca Book Publishers, as usual, trusted in me and supported me, even though the first pass at this story needed a lot of work. Thank you also to Christi Howes, who provided the much-needed editing.

Sylvia Olsen is a writer, storyteller and public speaker living on Vancouver Island in British Columbia. She is the author of several picture books and a number of first readers and novels for young adults, including *Murphy and Mousetrap* and *A Different Game*. She has also written one nonfiction book for adults. For more information, visit www.sylviaolsen.ca.